INDIANA and the
KINGDOM OF
THE CRYSTAL SKULL™

James Luceno

Based on the story by George Lucas and Jeff Nathanson
and the screenplay by David Koepp

LUCAS BOOKS

Scholastic Inc.

New York   Toronto   London   Auckland   Sydney
Mexico City   New Delhi   Hong Kong   Buenos Aires

ISBN-13: 978-0-545-00701-6
ISBN-10: 0-545-00701-1

12 11 10 9 8 7 6 5 4 3 2 1   8 9 10 11 12/0

Designed by Rick DeMonico
Printed in the U.S.A.
First printing, June 2008

Sometimes even the long empty stretches of Nevada's state highways could be dangerous places, especially for hapless prairie dogs when Jimmy "Quick Shift" Keegan was at the wheel of his hot rod. Peeling out from the gas station adjacent to the Atomic Café — the last gas for two hundred miles — Jimmy steered past the café's missile-shaped neon sign and fishtailed onto the pavement, the hot rod's fat rear tires flattening the earthen mound of a prairie dog that had sense enough to leap away in the nick of time.

Fueled on the burgers and fries served up by the Atomic Café's skinny cook, a dollar's worth of gas in the hot rod's tank — just over three gallons — and Jimmy was raring to go. Tommy Shiner sat beside him on the rolled-and-pleated red front seat; and in the plush rumble seat Jimmy's girlfriend Suzie and

and Tommy's new squeeze, Lindy, were yakking it up in the hot wind.

Jimmy's hot rod wasn't just any piece of vintage tin. The car was a black '32 Ford Roadster — twenty-five years old that summer — hoodless and roofless and hopped up, with four on the floor, oversized rear whitewalls for traction, and small front tires for enhanced handling. Good with his hands, Jimmy had lightened and lowered the body, bored out the engine, and modified the camshaft. The flathead shined like new, and its throaty exhaust purred through the custom pipes Jimmy had installed.

With no particular place to go this Saturday, the four teenagers were just joyriding to rock and roll blaring from the Roadster's chrome-knobbed radio. As Jimmy power-shifted up through the gears, Tommy twisted the radio's tuner to improve the reception. The few cars they passed were filled with tourists heading north from Las Vegas, and none of the drivers had showed any interest in challenging Jimmy to a race, but something was bound to turn up.

Coming around a bend in the highway, Jimmy spied a convoy of army vehicles stretched out in front of him — a couple of jeeps, canvas-topped trucks, and some kind of weapons transport, all of them painted a lusterless olive drab. Soldiers from one of the military bases or test facilities that had sprouted in the desert since the mines had closed and the local ranchers had sold off acreage to the government. Now and again, Jimmy would run into soldiers at the Atomic Café, sporting uniforms and crew cuts, sipping cups of Maxie's weak coffee. Seeing them, he'd ask himself why anyone would want to join up. Not that there were many options for a teenager living in Nevada in 1957. But there had to be more to life than learning to field-strip weapons and salute your superiors.

Given the Roadster's horsepower and the measured pace of the convoy, the half-dozen vehicles didn't present much of a challenge. *But what the heck,* Jimmy thought, *any chance to leave some rubber on the road and burn some gas.* He decided he would make his move just where the highway opened up, and take them well before the next bend. Reading his thoughts, Tommy reached over and shoved Jimmy's shoulder.

"Show 'em who's king of the road," Tommy encouraged.

"Floor it, Jimmy!" Lindy said.

Downshifting, Jimmy did just that. Veering the Roadster into the left lane, he gave it the gas, accelerating sharply past the weapons carrier and a couple of jeeps and trunks, Suzie and Lindy bouncing on the rumble seat in excitement and waving flirtatiously to the soldiers. Leading the convoy was a bullet-grille '51 Ford, as drab as the rest of the vehicles, except for a white star emblazoned on the driver's door, and capable of doing ninety or better on the straightaways. The soldier behind the wheel must have seen the Roadster racing up in the side-view mirror because just as Jimmy pulled even with him, the Ford leaped forward, determined not to be passed.

"Ford on Ford!" Tommy shouted into the wind. "Dust 'em, Jimbo!"

Jimmy glanced past Tommy to eyeball the staff car's driver — a sharp-featured guy a couple of years older than him, dressed in army fatigues, and clearly eager to race. Tightening his grip on the steering wheel, Jimmy set his jaw and studied the road ahead with renewed interest. A contest of any sort was a serious matter. Gunning the engine, he popped the clutch and jumped the Roadster into the lead — a lead just narrow enough to goad his opponent. Baited, the staff car surged forward, coming even with the Roadster, but only because Jimmy let it.

Suzie leaned forward, beaming. "Pedal to the metal!"

Yeah, Jimmy thought, *time to finish it.* He could tell that the soldier at the wheel of the staff car was already done with the race, anyway, easing off the gas and falling behind to allow the rest of the convoy to catch up. Still, there was no such thing as a minor win, and the best finish was a strong one. Slamming his foot on the accelerator, he shot the Roadster so far into the lead that the staff car might as well have been parked. Then, veering back into the right lane, he gave a wave and barreled off down the highway.

The uniformed driver of the Ford watched the kids race away, leaving the convoy to eat the Roadster's dust, two perky girls turning in their seats to blow good-bye kisses. *Just another group of spoiled teenagers,* the driver told himself. Under ordinary circumstances he wouldn't have allowed himself to be outraced by a freckle-faced punk at the wheel of a souped-up car, but this wasn't the time or place for such contests. There were far more pressing races that needed to be won.

The decision to back off from the challenge had fallen to the passenger in the front seat — a full-bird colonel, as shown by the insignia on his brimmed cap. The touch of the colonel's left hand on the driver's arm had put a quick end to the drag race. And now the colonel was gesturing with his square chin to a road that intersected the highway up ahead. Narrow but paved, the road wound up into a jumble of low, treeless hills before disappearing from sight.

The staff car driver swung the Ford off the highway, the vehicles that made up the convoy raising clouds of dust as they followed.

The secondary road was neither named nor identified by route markers, but signs of a different sort were affixed to the chain-link fencing that bordered it on both sides. *Restricted Area*, read one. *No trespassing or photography permitted.* The sign's fine print warned of dire consequences for any who failed to heed the directives. Farther along, dirt roads led north and south. The convoy snaked through a series of tight bends before climbing one of the hills, at the summit of which stood a formidable-looking sliding gate topped with barbwire. Alongside the gate was a small, shingled guard post, with a roof overhang that provided a patch of shade. From the building emerged three soldiers attired in Army fatigues, combat boots, and suspendered web belts. Two of them carried automatic rifles; the third, a sergeant, had a holstered .45 sidearm. All three wore helmets and armbands that designated them as security personnel.

The sergeant waved for the convoy to stop, and the staff car driver brought the Ford to a halt several feet from the gate. Loosing a meaningful exhale, the colonel opened the passenger-side door and stepped out. He was a tall man in fighting trim, with a face of planes and hollows that made him appear hostile even when he wasn't. Catching sight of his rank, the soldiers snapped to attention, the sergeant offering a crisp salute.

"Sorry, gentlemen, but this entire area is off-limits for

the next twenty-four hours for weapons testing. That includes all on-base personnel."

Without offering a response, the colonel continued toward the gate. Wary suddenly, the sergeant looked the colonel up and down.

"I'm afraid that the order applies to you, too, colonel — sir. CentCom sent out revised plans at oh-dark-thirty, this A.M." The noncom kept his voice courteous, but firm. He knew his duty, and wasn't about to surrender an inch of ground, even to a superior officer.

The colonel returned a tight-lipped smile, but kept right on walking. And the sergeant's earlier wariness blossomed into full-fledged suspicion.

"Sir?" he said questioningly, but his hand was already inching toward the holstered pistol.

The .45 was halfway out when three soldiers leaped from the rear of the covered truck, automatic rifles raised and trained on the trio of guards. The barrels of the weapons were fitted with sound suppressors, which seemed an odd touch out here in the desert, miles from anywhere, but the colonel hadn't known precisely what to expect and wanted to be prepared for any eventuality.

Rounds tore in muffled sibilance from the soldiers' rifles, and the three guards were blown off their feet. With silent efficiency — the result of months of planning and training — additional soldiers poured from the truck, some to strip the helmets and armbands from the dead guards, others to drag the bullet-ridden bodies across the pavement and into the guard house. While three soldiers slipped the pilfered items onto their heads and upper arms, others brought a crowbar to bear on the lock and thick chain that secured the gate.

Everyone except the three counterfeit guards clambered back into the vehicles, and when the gate slid open the convoy got under way, now with a palpable sense of urgency.

Over the rise, the dry country spread out in all directions. The area had been underwater in the distant past, and was now a vast salt flat.

Dominating the foreground was a windowless building, similar in appearance to a warehouse or an airplane hangar but built on a huge scale. An airstrip led directly up to the hangar, and a rail line ran into the salt flats from a smaller adjacent building. The numerals 5 and 1 were painted boldly on the hangar's enormous front doors.

No sooner did the convoy crunch to a stop in front of the doors than two soldiers jumped from the truck and hurried to a utility box that housed the controls for the doors. The colonel nodded to two soldiers who were standing alongside the truck, awaiting orders. Quickly the pair moved to the Ford staff car and popped the trunk. From the dark, spacious interior they hauled a blindfolded man to his feet. In his fifties, the man was thickly built and had a full head of graying brown hair. His several days' growth of whiskers, rumpled clothing, and assorted bruises told a story of rough treatment at someone's hands.

One of the soldiers drew a black-and-white photograph from his shirt pocket and placed it alongside the man's head, comparing the image to the reality.

"Not him," the colonel said. "Where's the professor?"

Once more the two soldiers reached into the trunk to drag into daylight a second man, a figure even more rumpled, battered, and bruised than the first.

CHAPTER TWO

*I*ndiana Jones' most recent memories — over the course of what he guessed was two days — consisted of being stuffed into one suffocating space after the next, always with proficiency, and typically with a good deal of gratuitous roughness. Plus, he had been blindfolded throughout and frequently gagged. He remembered the archaeological dig in Mexico, of course, because that's where he had been snatched from his tent in the middle of the night. He knew he had been in a plane since then, and in several trucks, and for the past couple of hours in the trunk of what could only be an American car, poor Mac gagged and bound beside him, taken from the same archaeological dig, where he had showed up only a day earlier to say hello, and was now caught up in whatever trouble Indy was in.

Indy still had no idea why he had been kidnapped or by whom. His captors had been careful to say as little as possible, so all of his attempts at eavesdropping had failed.

Certainly he had no shortage of enemies, going back to before his service in the war. Archaeology wasn't immune to rivalry, but archaeologists rarely resorted to violence against one another — at least not since René Belloq had died back in '36.

When Indy heard them pulling Mac from the trunk, then felt himself being hauled out, he thought for a moment that they were simply about to be transferred again. But no, there was something different in the air. The fact that they were removing his blindfold made it a certainty. This time they had arrived at their destination.

The glare of the sun made him squeeze his eyes shut, but even before he opened them he had a sense of the place. The air was hot and dry, and the breeze was gritty. A thought ran through his mind that he was still in Mexico. Ultimately his eyes told him otherwise. The distant painted mountains could have been those in Oaxaca, but they weren't. He was somewhere in the American Southwest. Not Utah, where he spent his teenage years, but New Mexico, perhaps. Or better yet, southern Nevada, in the salt flats area of Lincoln County.

Indy glanced at Mac, who was still squinting at the sky's brilliance and as wobbly on his feet as Indy. But what with all the punches they had taken and the two days of being bounced around, it was a miracle they could even stand. Most people knew Mac as George McHale, but to

Indy he had been Mac since day one. Their friendship went back more than fifteen years, before both of them had even been working for the military intelligence agencies of their respective nations: Mac for England's MI6, and Indy for the American OSS — the Office of Strategic Services.

When Indy looked past Mac to his captors, he began to blink again, this time in puzzlement. What in the world would the US Army want with him, and whatever it was, why couldn't they have simply asked? Indy regarded the enormous airplane hangar behind the soldiers. Numerals painted on its doors identified it as 51.

Then Indy heard something that made all his assumptions go up in smoke. The men he had taken for regular Army were conversing in Russian.

"Ruskies!" Mac said under his breath. "This won't be easy." His English accent made every line sound like the introduction to a joke.

Indy took in the jeeps and other vehicles. A group of Russians masquerading as Army soldiers at what had to be a government facility in southern Nevada. FBI Director J. Edgar Hoover, who saw Communists everywhere he looked, would have been thrilled.

"Not as easy as it used to be," Indy said finally.

One of the soldiers who had hauled Indy from the

trunk turned to him, but only to flatten Indy's battered old fedora down on his head. Indy saw that they had brought along his bullwhip and satchel bag as well, though his trusty revolver was nowhere to be seen.

"We've been through a lot worse than this," Mac was saying.

"Oh, yeah — when?"

"Flensburg, for starters," Mac said. "There were twice as many."

"We were a lot younger."

"Speak for yourself, mate. I'm still young."

Indy glanced at his bullwhip, which was coiled over the shoulder of one of the soldiers. "We had guns."

Mac only sniffed in theatrical derision. "Details. Five hundred bucks says we get out of this."

The words had scarcely left his mouth when the largest of the soldiers — masquerading as a colonel, no less — took a step in Mac's direction, removing his billed cap to reveal a nearly shaved skull and a sadistic expression.

"Make that one hundred," Mac said out of the corner of his mouth.

Indy managed a smile. Good ole Mac, always the optimist. He was about to say as much when a sedan arrived on the scene. As it did, the bogus colonel turned to face Indy. Tall and about as rugged-looking as they came, this was definitely the one who had pummeled him back in Quintana Roo, Indy told himself. For whatever reason, the guy had taken a liking to it.

The Russian gestured to the warehouse before stepping nose to nose with him. "You recognize this building, yes?"

"Get lost," Indy said.

Anticipating the punch, Indy took it on the side of the jaw and rolled with it, allowing his knees to buckle beneath him and dropping to his backside.

"Sorry," Indy said, working his jaw. "I meant to say, get lost, *comrade.*"

The Russian picked him up off the ground like he was a rag doll. He had one fist curled back to smash straight into Indy's nose when a woman's voice rang out.

"Prasteete!"

From the rear of the sedan stepped a slender figure who would have been more at home at the Bolshoi Ballet than in the salt flats of Nevada, despite the fact that she wore US Army attire. No older than thirty-five, she was tall and pale, and had jet-black hair, cut in bangs across the middle of her forehead and just touching the tops of her shoulders. At her side hung some sort of fencing sword in its scabbard.

The big Russian uncurled his fist, let go of Indy, and saluted curtly.

"At ease, Antonin Dovchenko," the woman told him, "as the Americans say." Regarding Indy, she added, "Where did you find him?"

"In Mexico," Dovchenko said, "digging in the dirt." He grabbed Indy's satchel — actually an old gas-mask bag — and began to empty the contents on the ground. "For this junk."

Indy watched in dismay as half a dozen Mayan figures and sacrificial plates smashed to pieces, the result of months of painstaking excavation.

Catching sight of Indy's frown, the Russian woman smiled lightly as she approached him. "Colonel Dovchenko has limited appreciation for ancient artifacts. But I am trying to educate him."

Indy held her gaze. "Let me guess. You're not from around here."

The woman's smile didn't falter. "You were described to me as an adventurer, Dr. Jones. A world traveler. So let us see you put your expertise to work in telling me where you imagine I'm from."

Indy studied her for a moment. "Well, the way you sink your pretty teeth into those W's, I'd say the Eastern Ukraine."

A blink betrayed her surprise. "Highest marks, Dr. Jones." She paused for a moment. "I am Dr. Irina Spalko. Three times I have received Order of Lenin, also medal as Hero of Socialist Labor, and why? Because I intuit things. I know them before anyone else, and what I do not know, I learn." Advancing a step, she tapped her forefinger against Indy's forehead. "And what I need to know now is in here."

Just then, electrical sparks began to fountain from the warehouse's main door power box, and from somewhere within the building came the sound of an outsize wheel rotating. Seconds later, the gargantuan doors rolled open, cleaving the numbers 5 and 1, and the Russians who had sprung the doors began to put away their tools.

Revealed, the interior of the place was enough to chill the heart of even the most conspicuous consumer. For as far as the eye could see and halfway to Hangar 51's fifty-foot-high trussed ceiling stood stack after stack of wooden packing crates, metal shipping containers, and overfilled dumpsters. Aisles as wide as city streets divided the towering stacks into rows, with illumination provided by hundreds of suspended light fixtures. Scattered about were cardboard boxes of every size and geometrical shape imaginable, bins and barrels filled to their brim with machine parts, paper bags stuffed with dossiers, bulging attaché cases, pieces of furniture, and components from airplanes, cars, boats, and who knew what else. It was like someone's idea of a storage unit nightmare.

Indy, Mac, and the Russians gaped in amazement.

Then two of the soldiers pressed the muzzles of their automatic weapons into Indy's and Mac's backs and began to prod them into motion. Some of the jeeps and trucks followed them inside.

Looking at Indy, Spalko gestured broadly. "This is where your government hides its military treasures, yes?"

"All I know is it's a warehouse," Indy said. "I've never been here before."

Spalko smiled in a way that told him she didn't buy a word of it. "Object we seek: rectangular storage container. Dimensions: two meters by one meter by two hundred centimeters. Contents of box are highly magnetized. The crate is no doubt familiar to you."

Indy shook his head in equal disbelief. "I have no idea what you're talking about. And that's got nothing to do with the way you're butchering our language."

Spalko paused to fix her gaze on him, as if he were an insect pushpinned to a specimen pad. Indy didn't blink, not even once, and Spalko was the first to avert her eyes.

"You're a hard man to read, Dr. Jones. So perhaps it is best that we do this the old-fashioned way." Spalko's voice took on a hard edge. "You will tell us. You will help us find what we seek."

Indy snorted a laugh. "Listen, sister, even if I knew what you —"

Deftly, Spalko drew a rapier from the scabbard and pressed the tip to Indy's throat.

Indy looked at the slender blade askance, then cut his eyes to Spalko. "Killing me isn't going to solve your problem."

She thought about it and nodded. "You're right."

As quickly as the sword had been raised to Indy's throat, the butt of a rifle slammed into Mac's gut, doubling him over. Taking hold of Mac's arms, two soldiers dragged him across the cement floor to where one of the trucks was idling, dropping him so that his head was positioned in direct line of the rear tires.

Spalko shouted something in Russian, and Indy heard the truck driver grind the gear box into reverse.

She looked hard at Indy. "I say once more, Dr. Jones, you *will* help us locate the container!"

CHAPTER THREE

*I*ndy threw his hands up, palms facing outward in a placating gesture. "Okay, okay!"

On Spalko's command, the truck stopped, its rear tire inches from Mac's head.

Indy's thoughts whirled. "This crate you're looking for . . . you say it's about the size of a coffin, but thinner." He glanced around in mounting agitation. "Jeez, there must be a thousand crates that size in here!" He looked at Mac. "Don't worry, buddy." Then he looked at Spalko. "Highly magnetized, right? Okay, then what we've gotta do is look for signs of the magnetic field." He swung to Dovchenko. "I need a compass." When the Russian only stared in bewilderment, he went on: "You know: north, south, east . . . Gah, no wonder it took you people so many years to send the Nazis packing."

"Jones!" Spalko snapped.

"All right, take it easy," Indy said. With the Russians

and Mac in tow, he began to hurry down one of the aisles that separated the stacks, his eyes searching for any signs of magnetic activity. He hooked a right into another aisle, then another, the stacks towering over him as tall as farm silos. He made a left, another left, a right. And just then . . . Were his eyes deceiving him or were the locks on those crates tilted ever so slightly in one direction?

Stopping suddenly, he pointed to Dovchenko. "Rounds! I need a couple of rounds from your pistol."

Dovchenko gaped at him, then laughed — but only until Spalko ordered him to obey Indy's request. Drawing his sidearm, Dovchenko removed the clip and pressed three rounds into Indy's palm.

"Toolbox!" Indy said, like a surgeon barking orders to a scrub nurse. And in seconds, one of the technicians who had worked on the door controls was hurrying forward, already unsnapping the box's lid.

Indy fished around inside the box until he located a pair of pliers, and with those he twisted the rounds from their casings and dumped the gunpowder from them into the palm of his left hand.

Aware of Spalko's interest, he said, "If the thing you're looking for is really as magnetized as you say, then the metal in the gunpowder should . . ."

Indy interrupted himself to blow the pile of gunpowder from his palm. The particles dispersed, but only for a moment. Then they began to coalesce in midair, as if in allegiance to some unseen force. When the cloud finally settled to the concrete floor it assumed the shape of a line.

". . . point the way," Indy completed.

Allowing her eagerness to show, Spalko raced into the mouth of the aisle in front of everyone else. "Which crate?" she said, eyeing the stacks in sudden alarm. "Which crate?"

Indy ran his hand down his face. *Think!* he told himself. His gaze fell on the shotgun one of the soldiers carried. "Pellets," he said, mostly to himself. "I need shells."

The soldier looked to Spalko for permission, then ejected a cartridge from the breech of the shotgun and handed it over. Indy didn't bother looking for a tool; he simply bit the cardboard cartridge in half and emptied the shot onto the floor. The pellets bounced and began to roll away, slowly at first, but gaining speed as they moved down the aisle, with Indy, Mac, and the rest running to keep up. Indy reached the base of a particularly precarious mound of crates in time to see the pellets roll *up* the mound's vertical face and disappear into the space between two crates in the middle.

Climbing partway up, Indy shouted for someone to give him a hand extricating the crate from the pile, and Dovchenko stepped forward, puffed up like a circus strongman. Two soldiers joined in, and in moments the four of them were tossing crates aside in an effort to reach the one the shotgun pellets had entered. Landing on the hard floor, some of the crates burst open, revealing bundles of dossiers marked EYES ONLY and manila envelopes bulging with surveillance photographs.

Hurling boxes and bins from the stack, Indy noticed a cluster of shotgun pellets quivering on the side of a crate that matched the one Spalko had described. A faded label stenciled on the side of the crate read: —*SWELL, N.M. 7-9-47*. In spite of himself, Indy grinned. He hadn't seen the crate before, but he knew that "—swell, N.M." could only be Roswell, New Mexico. But when he looked to Spalko for some sign of approbation, she wouldn't even grant him a smile.

Even before the crate was lowered fully to the floor, the hands of the Russians' cheap wristwatches were spinning madly. Snatching a crowbar from one of the soldiers, Spalko threw herself into the task of prying loose the wooden slates that made up the lid.

"*Moyo zolotse*," she said to no one in particular as the lid came away.

The crate enclosed a rectangular stainless-steel coffin that more closely resembled a containment tank of some sort. But that wasn't the end of it. Pressurized, the steel container released a blue-tinged gas into the air on being opened. Revealed inside was what looked to be a metallic body bag for a diminutive creature.

Ordered by Spalko to open the bag, a soldier leaned over the steel container, only to watch in awe as his timepiece flew from his wrist to adhere to the wrapping. Indy caught a quick glimpse of the impression the small body had left in the foil.

Arms akimbo, Spalko stood to her full height, smiling in self-satisfaction.

"Do you still deny, Dr. Jones, that you had this crate brought here, so that your government could conduct experiments on their find?" Suddenly she stopped, almost as if alerted, and whirled to the soldiers in warning.

But the warning arrived a moment too late.

Indy had taken advantage of the Russians' distraction to grab his bullwhip from the shoulder of the soldier guarding him. Now he rammed his own shoulder into the soldier with enough force to send him flying backwards across the floor. At once, the soldier guarding Mac pivoted toward Indy, but only to encounter the leather thong of the bullwhip, which wrapped around his weapon, and, at the flick of Indy's wrist, caused it to fire. Rounds ripped from the barrel straight into the Russian Indy had shouldered backwards. A second flick of Indy's wrist dragged the soldier into Indy's free arm, and in an instant Indy had disarmed the man and tossed his weapon to Mac. Hurling the soldier into Spalko, Indy raced to retrieve the weapon of the Russian who had been shot.

Those soldiers who were still standing tried to draw a bead on Indy, but by the time they did Indy and Mac were positioned back to back with their weapons raised, holding everyone at bay. Indy traversed his weapon until he had Spalko in his sights.

"Guns down! Put 'em down or the Colonel Doctor is dead."

Following Dovchenko's lead, the soldiers began to lower their rifles and sidearms. But just then, something odd happened. Spalko smiled, and the rest raised their weapons once more. Indy turned to see Mac's gun aimed at his head.

Indy had to gulp to find his voice. "Mac, why?"

Mac shrugged in nonchalance. "What can I tell you, mate? I'm a born capitalist. And they paid me well."

CHAPTER FOUR

*I*ndy shook his head in disbelief. "After all the years we spent spying on the Reds? Are you kidding me?"

Mac placed himself among the soldiers. "Had a run of bad luck, mate. Legendarily bad luck. Can't go home empty-handed all my life."

Grinning in menace, Dovchenko stepped forward, chambering a round in his handgun.

"No defiant last words, Dr. Jones?" Spalko asked as Dovchenko leveled his weapon at Indy's head.

Indy showed her a lopsided grin. "I like Ike."

"Drop the gun," Dovchenko said.

Indy nodded. "You got it."

But instead of merely setting the automatic rifle down, he pitched it into the air. Seconds later, it slammed to the floor angrily enough to spit bullets in all directions, one of the first of which ripped through the boot of one of the soldiers, blowing off his toes. Loosing a pained scream, the soldier began to hop about, his finger tightening on the trigger of his automatic. Rounds spewed into the air, ripping into some crates and ricocheting from others. Dodging the spray, Indy scampered to the top of the closest stack, searching desperately for an avenue of escape.

Wood splintering around him, he began to leap from stack to stack, dodging fire from soldiers who had emerged into the open. Below him off to one side, he saw Spalko gesturing for the Roswell crate to be moved into the back of one of the jeeps.

His lips a thin line, Indy watched the jeep screech off. Glancing up, he fixed his aim on one of the dangling light fixtures, and, with a flick of his wrist, coiled the business end of the bullwhip around the power cord that connected the button-shaped fixture to an electric box on a ceiling beam. Not a moment before his perch was reduced to sawdust by a hail of rifle fire, he swung out over the heads of the stunned soldiers in pursuit of Spalko's jeep, like Tarzan clinging to a jungle vine.

His target was almost directly below him when he reached the highest point of his arc. But a slight miscalculation landed him not in the rear of the jeep but on its rear hatch, where he teetered for a moment before falling backwards onto the hood of a jeep directly behind Spalko's, his whip unraveling as he fell. A somersault landed him groaning in pain in the front seat, and smack between two startled soldiers who were even more surprised to hear him say, "Darn, that looked closer."

Punching the driver in the face and slamming an elbow into the midsection of the soldier in the passenger seat, he sent both men flying from the jeep and planted himself at the steering wheel. Spalko's jeep had a good lead, but not for long. Calling all power from the engine, Indy roared off, skidding around corners and accelerating on the straightaways. Catching up, he used the jeep as a weapon to batter Spalko's, sending it head on into the base of a stack of crates. Momentum carried Spalko clear over the hood of the smashed vehicle, and by the time she picked herself up off the floor, Indy was racing away in her jeep and with the steel container.

Barreling into an intersection, Indy chanced to see the staff car bearing down on him from the right. A glance in the rearview mirror revealed that one of the trucks was closing on him from behind. Born of a split-second decision, Indy threw the jeep into a screeching right-hand turn, effectively playing chicken with the approaching sedan. Behind him, the truck swerved into the intersecting aisle and began to narrow the lead Indy had on it. The aisle left no room for fancy maneuvers, but a latticework of ceiling girders did. Once more the bullwhip cracked, entwining itself around one of the beams and lifting Indy straight out of the jeep.

Below him, brakes screamed in protest. The sedan impacted the front of the now-driverless jeep at the same instant the truck plowed into the rear end, crushing the thing like a tin can and redirecting the Russians' vehicles into stacks of crates on both sides of the aisle. Avalanching to the floor, several of the crates burst open. Indy was stupefied to see a cherubim-crowned golden chest packed in one of them.

The Ark of the Covenant. The vaunted prize in a quest that had pitted him against Belloq and the Nazis in 1936. Indy and Marion Ravenwood . . .

"So *this* is where it ended up," he said. Recalling what federal agents had told him at the time, he muttered: "Top men are working on it. . . ."

He barely had time for a grunt of disenchantment when a fusillade of rounds punched holes in everything around him. Lowering himself to the floor, he whirled and ran, even while Mac — picking his way out of the wreckage of truck, jeep, and sedan — was yelling for him to stop.

Glimpsing an exit ahead, Indy shot for it at full speed. He wasn't halfway there when a jeep lunged straight into him from a side aisle, lifting him over the engine compartment and into the windshield. Behind the glass on the driver's side was none other than Dovchenko, blind with rage — and suddenly blinded by Indy's bulk. Twisting the steering wheel to avoid colliding with an overturned crate, the Russian sent the jeep bouncing down a long flight of concrete steps and smack into a cement block wall.

Moaning, Indy rolled from the hood to the floor. His peripheral vision told him that they had bounced down into an underground bunker and he could see train tracks. Before he knew what was happening, Dovchenko grabbed hold of him and hurled him up onto the deck of a railroad flat car. Except this wasn't an ordinary flat car. In place of wheels the car was attached to the track by pads that curved around the head of the rails.

The flat car sat at the start of train tracks that led off into a dark tunnel. Fastened to the bed of the car was a jet engine, into whose control panel Indy had inadvertently careened as a result of the Russian's powerful throw. Just as the stars were fading from Indy's vision, a red light flashed on the control panel and a repetitive buzz began to sound from distant speakers. Illumination panels came to life in the tunnel, and a door shuddered open.

That was as much as Indy knew before Dovchenko pounced on him again and sent him sailing across the bed of the flat car. Scrambling to his feet, Indy managed to slug him in the face. But the Russian only laughed it off before clamping his hands around Indy's neck and squashing him against the curved side of the jet engine. With supreme effort, Indy twisted his shmooshed face to one side, but only to greet more bad news. Hobbling down the stairs came Mac, with several soldiers in his wake, and through a doorway that accessed the bunker howled a jeep carrying three more soldiers.

Dovchenko, meanwhile, was clearly intent on choking the life out of Indy, whose face was already turning blue. Twisting his head in the opposite direction, Indy saw that his foot was just inches from what appeared to be the jet engine's throttle. By extending his leg he was just able to give it a solid kick.

Against even Indy's expectations, the engine roared to life, emitting a blade of rippling white fire that scorched the bed of the flat car and blew the arriving jeep to smithereens, incinerating the trio of soldiers.

At the foot of the concrete staircase, Mac and the other soldiers recoiled from the intense heat and shrapnel. When at last they dared to look, they saw the flat car streaking down the tunnel, bound for the salt flats, taking Indy and Dovchenko with it.

In Hangar 51, Irina Spalko used her fingertips to comb back her black hair, as contingents of soldiers arrived in her staff car and perhaps the sole remaining jeep. Just then, from somewhere outside the hangar, a deafening boom shattered the silence.

A sonic boom.

"Follow the tracks," she barked to the soldiers in the vehicles. "Find him and bring him to me."

She would have preferred giving the order to kill Jones, but she needed him.

She had heard that Jones was trouble, an extraordinary nuisance, and thus far he was living up to his legend. She had heard, too, that more often than not he had come out on top, though she suspected that his many successes owed to his never having confronted an equal. Until now.

Jones's weakness was his single-mindedness. He was essentially a retriever — big and dopey, but very skilled. One simply had to give him a whiff of something and he would be off and running, facing down all odds until he had found the object. More important, he was driven by instincts that superseded nationalism, religion, even morality at times. He was a purebred seeker, but like any obedient dog, he could be taught a new trick. Soon enough Spalko's obsession would become his. It all came down to baiting him, then undermining him.

Like most Americans, Jones was so enslaved to the pursuit of personal freedom and happiness that he had lost sight of life's higher purpose and humanity's potential to evolve. He was incapable of understanding the power of the collective mind, that the whole was greater than the sum of its separate parts. But he would learn.

She had intuited all of this when she stared into his eyes. She liked that he was psychically strong, a true challenge. But she would break him. Once she had the object, he would be putty in her hands.

She refused to accept that he knew nothing about the object, or that he was as guileless as he wanted everyone to believe. Either Jones knew where the object was, or, given the right bait, he could be induced to locate it.

Premier Khrushchev wasn't as infatuated with psychism as Joseph Stalin had been. But once the object was found, Khrushchev's eyes would be opened as well.

Spalko watched the jeep and the sedan speed off in pursuit of Jones. American soldiers would be showing up before too long, she thought. The time had come for the Russians to disappear.

CHAPTER FIVE

*T*he jet engine Indy enabled had turned the flat car into a rocket sled, and now it was tearing down the railroad tracks going a couple of hundred miles an hour. In constant danger of being vaporized by the engine's propulsive fire, Indy and Dovchenko were hanging on for dear life, g-forces all but peeling their faces from their skulls. The distant hills that rimmed the salt flat were a blur, but through the wind-summoned tears pouring from Indy's eyes, he could see that the flat car was running out of track — and fast. He tried to imagine what it was going to feel like to plow into the scabrous ground at supersonic speed, but quickly realized he was better off not imagining it.

Just when death seemed inevitable, the engine suddenly changed tunes, quieting from a roar to an almost gentle purr, its hot-blue flame going from steady to intermittent. The flat car began to decelerate, and the facial features of its two wretched passengers took on a semblance of normalcy.

Ultimately the engine shut down completely, leaving the flat car to glide to a placid halt at a bumper erected at the end of the tracks, alongside a small monitoring station. Staggering to their feet, Indy and Dovchenko faced off like drunken sailors, huffing and puffing, throwing wild punches that missed by a mile. Seconds into the dizzy fray, Dovchenko simply collapsed onto the bed of the car, and Indy rolled off its edge like a sack of potatoes. When his head finally cleared, he looked back toward the warehouse, his crossed eyes gradually zeroing in on twin plumes of dust on the horizon.

The Russians, he thought. So much for them leaving him alone now that they had the crate. He fixed his gaze on a nearby ridge of low hills, and on shaky legs set out for it.

As foreseen, a US Army unit had arrived at Hangar 51. The soldiers were just beginning to probe the interior, but Spalko wasn't concerned. She had planned for this eventuality, and should it come to having to engage in a firefight, then so be it. Three members of her group had already been burned to a crisp in a subterranean bunker.

She had the crate relocated to the backseat of the

crumpled sedan that would have to serve as a getaway car. The Englishman that Jones called Mac had the wheel. In a fit of anger, he had ripped the mangled hood from the vehicle.

Throwing the car into gear, Mac was ready to depart when one of Spalko's soldiers hurried to the passenger-side window.

"Colonel Dovchenko has been found — alive — at the end of the railroad tracks," the soldier said. "The professor is gone, but his boots have left a clear trail."

"Then find him!" Spalko said. "If he resists, kill him."

Mac glanced at her. "You think that's wise at this point?"

Spalko blew out her breath. "Find him," she repeated to the soldier. "Then I'll decide what to do with him."

She nodded to Mac, and he slammed his foot down on the accelerator pedal.

The sun was going down when Indy saw it, not believing his eyes at first, certain it was a mirage, like an oasis seen by a dehydrated Foreign Legionnaire. But the closer he came to his destination the more confident he grew that it was not an optical illusion after all.

It was a town. More, it was perfect town, of the sort only Americans could build, with a grid of perfect streets lined with perfect little homes fronted by perfectly kept lawns and lit from within by perfect little lamps and flickering television sets.

Refusing to acknowledge the aches and pains that plagued him, Indy hastened his pace. It struck him as odd how the town just sort of *began* out of nowhere, but the thought didn't slow him any. Hurrying down a paved street, he glanced at the houses to both sides of him. Towns just didn't come any quieter than this one. It wasn't even dark and the sidewalks had already been rolled up. Not a car cruising, not a pedestrian in sight —

He froze in his tracks. Speeding through an intersection two blocks away was a military jeep, two Russians in front, one in the rear.

"Nuts," Indy said quietly.

He cut left onto the first side street and began to trot, calling for help, but not entirely surprised when no doors opened. With his week's growth of beard and filthy clothes, he figured he had to look like a prospector who'd spent one too many months in the desert. He cut left again, into a driveway this time, then through a backyard where he nearly garroted himself on a clothesline. Disentangling himself from freshly laundered items, he made straight for the back door of the nearest house, letting himself in when no one responded to his urgent raps on the jamb.

He found himself in a perfect little wallpapered kitchen equipped with a Formica-topped table, wood cabinets, and the very latest in appliances, including a spotless white refrigerator that looked as if it was capable of making snow.

"Anyone home?" he called out.

Music of a sort drew him into a living room, where a family of four was sitting in obvious fascination on a curved couch in front of a small black-and-white television tuned at the moment to *The Howdy Doody Show*, whose "Ta-ra-ra-boom-de-ay" theme song was issuing from the set's tiny speaker.

"Darn," Indy muttered, dismayed by the family's rapt attention.

Spying a telephone, he lifted the handset and jabbed at the button on the receiver. "Operator," he said. "Operator! Russian spies! Here, in your town! They broke into a . . ."

He let his words trail off. For some reason, the line was dead.

"Don't you people have a phone that works?" he said to Howdy's mesmerized Peanut Gallery. But not one of them even turned to him. "What's wrong with you people? Has television got you that brainwashed? Have the body snatchers been in town?" Crossing the room in sudden anger, he grabbed hold of the father's arm, yanking it *right out of its shirt sleeve*!

He gawked at the thing, even after revelation struck. The arm was plastic! The mom and the kids were plastic! They were mannequins.

"Why, Howdy," Buffalo Bob Smith was saying on the set, "haven't you guessed yet? You're in an imaginary place."

A wailing siren brought Indy back to his senses. Listening for a moment, he said, "That's not just any siren —"

He burst through the front door onto the lawn. A 1957 red-and-white Chevy was parked in the driveway, alongside a child's scooter. A mannequin mailman stood at the mailbox, and across the street a mannequin Good Humor man handed out ice cream bars to mannequin children. Up the block a woman walked a mannequin dog. In the neighbor's yard, a group of mannequin youths sat on bikes, while a mannequin woman waved from the steering wheel of a motionless Buick.

Meanwhile, the siren continued to blare in warning.

"Oh, this isn't good," Indy said in mounting panic. "This isn't good at all!"

He pivoted through a circle, his gaze falling on a sign that should have read Mayberry or Smallville or the name of some other classic American town. But this sign read: DOOM TOWN. U.S. NEVADA PROVING GROUND. CIVILIANS TURN BACK!

The siren fell silent momentarily, and a voice boomed from nearby loudspeakers. "All monitoring personnel take final positions. Countdown is initiated. Detonation commencing in T-minus one minute."

Indy's jaw dropped, and he began to run — in circles initially, then straight down the street. He was just rounding the closest corner when dirt began to geyser at his feet, and he heard the reports of an automatic weapon. Looking up, he saw a Russian soldier rushing toward him. Whirling one-hundred-and-eighty degrees, Indy found the jeep screeching to a halt in front of him, the soldier in the passenger seat leveling his gun.

"T-minus forty-five seconds," the loudspeaker voice announced.

Indy raised his hands to the soldiers in a gesture of surrender. "Wait! Stop!" he said, trusting that they knew at least a few words of English. "Don't you realize what this is — where we are?"

He motioned to the houses and pedestrians. "They're all *fake*! None of this is real!" He pointed over the roof of one of the tiny structures. Even in the growing dark it was possible to make out the top of a tall, guyed tower, festooned with siren horns and loudspeakers.

And suspended from a thick platform at the summit: a couple of kilotons of nuclear bomb.

The eyes of the three Russians opened as wide as

Indy's, panicked shrieks tearing from their throats. The driver of the jeep gunned the motor and peeled out, streaking past Indy and stopping only long enough to snag the third soldier before speeding off.

Indy chased them briefly, then, realizing the futility of it, stopped, planting his hands on his knees and laughing maniacally. "Sure, don't bother to wait for me!"

"T-minus thirty seconds and counting," boomed the voice.

Gritting his teeth in determination, Indy executed an about-face and raced back to the house he left only moments earlier. He dashed through the draped living room, where the cheery Howdy Doody music was still wafting from the television, and skidded to a halt in the kitchen. He ran his fingers over lettering on the refrigerator door: *Lead-lined for superior insulation.*

"T-minus fifteen seconds and counting," the voice said.

Climbing into a refrigerator had its own dangers. But Indy hadn't braved the wrath of God and Kali and the Grail temple's trio of challenges to end his days as a smudge of irradiated dust.

"T-minus ten seconds and counting."

Throwing open the refrigerator door, he began pulling the contents onto the linoleum floor — food, bottles of milk, shelves, drawers, everything he could tear loose. And then he began cramming himself inside.

"Any fallout shelter in a storm," he said.

"T-minus five seconds and counting."

He tried pulling the door closed, but it wouldn't seal.

Realizing that his bomber jacket was blocking the latch, he yanked at it, just managing to get the door sealed as the loudspeaker voice was counting down to one.

A moment of stillness settled over Doom Town. Then the night sky glared with such ferocity that the world turned completely white. A thick column of nuclear conflagration descended from the sky, flattening out as it struck the earth and spreading outward in a disk of roiling fire. Caught up in the inferno, houses imploded, cars melted, and mannequins disintegrated. Sand was turned to glass and shadows were burned into the ground.

A mile away, the jeep was running full out when the leading edge of the bomb's shock wave overtook it, slagging the vehicle and vaporizing its three Russian passengers. If, in the instant before the blast cloud struck, they had glanced to the right, they might have seen a white refrigerator whiz past them, surfing the unholy current.

Far from what had been the edge of town, the refrigerator plowed into the soft ground at the base of a hill.

Airborne debris raining down around it, the blackened and partly melted appliance made pinging sounds as it cooled. Finally the door opened, and smoke curled from the interior, followed by a dazed and confused Indiana Jones, who staggered from the scorched thing like a zombie risen from a grave. In the distance, and to Indy's utter horror, a cloud of fuming incandescence was mushrooming into the night sky.

Lit from within, the churning globular cloud bore an eerie similarity to a human skull.

CHAPTER SIX

Rescued by an Army patrol, Indy stood in the decon-
tamination room of a Nevada Test Site monitoring station,
twenty miles from Doom Town, while a technician passed
the wand of a Geiger counter over his bruised, battered,
and now hosed and scrubbed-down body. The counter
emitted a couple of beeps, but the technician assured him
that he had nothing to worry about.

"Sure, what's a bit of radiation poisoning, huh?"

The technician studied him for a moment. "Hey, pal,
at least you're alive."

Two men dressed in dark suits and thin ties were waiting for him in an adjoining room. Indy had encountered
their type too many times over the course of the years. The
pair had refused to say just which federal agency they
worked for, but Indy's money would have been on the FBI.
The taller of the two had introduced himself as Smith; the
other one was Taylor.

Waving Indy into a straight-backed chair, Smith accepted a sheet of teletype from a soldier and took a moment to read it.

"Your story appears to check out, Dr. Jones," he said at last. "But I'm still mystified as to why you were in the Russian car in the first place."

"Like I told you," Indy said, "I was knocked unconscious and kidnapped from an archaeological dig in Mexico. I woke up in the trunk of the car."

"Clever cover story," Taylor said.

Indy glanced at him. "Yeah, and I wanted to make it sound convincing by sitting through an atomic blast."

"So you were kidnapped along with your good friend, George McHale," Smith said.

"Former friend," Indy said with distaste. "I had no reason to suspect Mac was a spy. We served together in the war. Mac was MI6 when I was with the OSS. We must have gone on twenty or thirty missions together in Europe and the Pacific."

"The way I heard it," Smith interrupted, "Donovan's outfit was rife with Commies."

Indy stared at him. "You're barking up the wrong tree, buster."

"Don't wave your war record in our face, Colonel Jones," Taylor said. "We all played our parts."

"That's retired colonel," Indy said. "And just whose side were you on?"

Smith and Taylor traded looks; then Smith said, "Maybe you fail to grasp the gravity of your situation, Dr. Jones. You aided and abetted KGB operatives by breaking into a top secret military installation, right in the heart of the United States of America. My country."

Indy refused to take the bait. "What was inside the steel container they took?"

"You tell us," Taylor said. "You've seen it before."

Indy snorted. "You mean that Air Force fiasco in forty-seven? They tossed me and about twenty other people into a bus with blacked-out windows. We weren't allowed to speak to one another. They drove us to a spot in the middle of nowhere, where some sort of recovery mission was in progress. Some sort of experimental craft had crashed. I remember small corpses wrapped in magnetic shrouds. We were never given the full story. The Air Force brass threatened us with treason if we asked questions or spoke to anyone about what we'd seen." Indy looked at Smith. "Your turn. *You* tell *me* what was in the box."

Smith shook his head. "It's classified."

"I still have my clearance," Indy said.

"This process works best when we ask the questions, Dr. Jones," Taylor said.

Indy leaned forward in the chair. "Mummified remains of a spaceman?"

Taylor smiled without showing his teeth. "We have no records of any such 'spaceman,' as you call it."

"You must be confused, Dr. Jones," Smith said. "After all you've been through."

"Hangar Fifty-one is merely a storage facility for B-series aircraft components."

"Sure it is," Indy said flatly.

Just then the door to the room flew back on its hinges, and a broad-shouldered Army general entered. "Indy, thank goodness you're all right! Don't you know better than to climb into a refrigerator? Those things can be death traps!"

Indy grinned. His friendship with General Robert Ross went back more than a decade. "Good to see you, too, Bob."

Ross looked at Smith and Taylor. "Relax, boys. I'll vouch for Dr. Jones' loyalty to the US of A."

Indy turned to Ross. "What's going on? KGB agents on US soil? There was a colonel named Dovchenko, but who was that woman?"

Smith and Taylor exchanged looks of concern. "Describe her," Taylor said.

"Tall, black hair, in her mid-thirties," Indy said. "She carried some kind of sword — a rapier, I think. Knew how to use it, too."

Smith and Taylor exchanged a look — Indy thought they may have recognized the description. Then, in a rush, Taylor excused himself and left the room.

General Ross looked amazed. "Irina Spalko?" he asked.

Smith pulled a file from his briefcase, rifled through it, and handed Indy a surveillance photograph of Irina Spalko.

"Yeah, that's her," Indy said. "What's the big deal?"

Ross spoke while Smith replaced the photo. "She was Joseph Stalin's fair-haired girl. His favorite scientist, if you can call psychic research science. Khrushchev isn't as enamored of her, but Spalko has been given his blessing to scour the world for artifacts that might have military applications. You know, paranormal stuff —"

"Some things never change," Indy muttered.

"General Ross," Smith said, "I think you've said more than enough."

Ross gave him an icy look. "Not everyone in the Army is a Communist, Paul. No matter what your director thinks. And certainly not Indy."

Indy turned to Smith. "What exactly am I being charged with, other than surviving a nuclear bomb?"

"Nothing yet," Smith said as Taylor was reentering the room. "But frankly, Dr. Jones, your close association with George McHale calls into question all your activities, including some of your actions during the war."

Ross shook his head in disbelief. "Are you nuts? You know how many medals this son-of-a-gun has earned?"

"It's more a matter of whether he deserves them," Smith said.

"Let's say for now that you are a person of interest to the Bureau," Taylor said.

"Of great interest," Smith couldn't help but add.

Indy grew serious. "Look, if you have doubts about me, call Congressman Freleng. Or Abe Portman, in Army Intel. Heck, ask anybody. I've got lots of friends in Washington."

Taylor smiled thinly. "I think, professor, you'll find you might be wrong about that."

CHAPTER SEVEN

*A*utumn had come early to Connecticut. On the campus of Marshall College, green was reserved for the ivy that clung to the stone and brick walls of the buildings. Elsewhere the colors were maple red, chestnut yellow, oak brown. But the cool, sunny weather belied a gloomy undercurrent. Indy had sensed it in the air since his return from Nevada several days earlier. Dressed in his tweed suit and wire-rim bifocals, he stood at the blackboard of the class he taught in field archaeology, lecturing by rote about grooved pottery from Skara Brae, and some of the students responded with yawns. When the door to the classroom opened and Dean Stanforth poked his head in, Indy knew that trouble had caught up with him.

"May I have a moment, professor? I need to speak to you," Stanforth said. A tall man with silvering hair, he wore a stylish suit and expensive wing-tipped shoes.

"Can it wait? I'm almost done."

Stanforth shook his head. "Sorry."

Indy set his piece of chalk on the blackboard shelf and turned to the class, his hands flat on a counter crowded with pieces of ancient pottery, masks, statues, and fetishes.

"Uh, read the section where Michaelson discusses his findings," he told the class. "I won't be a minute."

He went to the door, opened it, and stepped into the corridor, where he found Stanforth pacing in agitation.

"What?" Indy said. When the dean began to hem and haw, Indy cut him off. "Give it to me straight, Charlie."

Stanforth shook his head in consternation. "FBI agents showed up this morning. They ransacked your office, searched all your files —"

"And you let them?" Indy fumed. "You're the dean, for cryin' out loud. They had no right."

"I'm afraid they had every right. They had search warrants. The university can't afford to become embroiled in this kind of controversy — not in the current political climate."

Indy ran his hand down his face. "So you're firing me?"

"You have no idea of the pressure I'm under from the board of regents. But in any case, you're not being fired, exactly. An indefinite leave of absence. You'll continue to receive your full salary for —"

"I don't want their money," Indy snapped. "You wanna know where they can deposit their money?"

Stanforth made a calming gesture. "Be reasonable. Think of this as a . . . sabbatical."

"Sabbatical," Indy said, laughing without merriment. "Right."

Stanforth's shoulders sagged. "You don't know what I had to go through to get that much for you."

"What you went through?" Indy laughed again. "What exactly did you have to go through, Charlie?"

Stanforth looked at him. "I resigned."

Later that same day, in the bedroom of Indy's on-campus home, Indy pulled articles of clothing from the closet and the bureau drawers while Stanforth, slouched in Indy's desk chair, worked at finishing the bottle they had opened earlier. On the bed sat a worn leather suitcase.

"Where will you go?" Stanforth asked while he watched Indy pack.

Indy paused for a moment. "Train to New York, overnight to London, for starters. Maybe I'll end up teaching in Leipzig. Heinrich owes me a favor."

Stanforth considered it. "I suppose there's nothing to

keep you here." When Indy shook his head, he added: "I don't blame you. The way you're being treated. Sometimes I scarcely recognize this country anymore. First, people like McCarthy, and now Hoover, they've got us seeing Communists in our soup. When the hysteria reaches academia, I guess it's time to call it a career."

Indy looked at him. "How'd Deirdre take the news of your resignation?"

"How does any wife take such things? With equal parts pride and panic."

Indy exhaled. "I feel like a heel for what I said, Charlie. I shouldn't have doubted you for a second."

Stanforth shrugged it off. "You have every good reason to question even your best friends these days."

Indy sat on the edge of the bed. "Brutal couple of years, Charlie. My dad, then Marcus Brody. . . . Now Mac may as well be dead."

Stanforth nodded in commiseration. "We seem to have reached the age where life begins to take more than it gives."

Indy fell silent for a moment, then bolted to his feet and resumed packing. Stanforth reached for the bottle.

"Maybe just another half a glass . . ."

Indy moved to the desk and began sorting through papers, tossing some into a wastebasket, others — including his passport — onto the bed.

"I wish that someone like Deirdre had come into your life, Indy, to help you through times like these," Stanforth was saying. "Or maybe someone did and you didn't realize it at the time."

Indy glanced at him. "Let's not tug on that thread right now, okay, pal?"

Stanforth nodded, then glanced at his wristwatch. "Good Lord, I've got to get home. Don and Maggie are driving *spousum et familia* up from the city for dinner. Emergency council meeting."

Indy smiled. "They're good kids, Charlie. You're a lucky man."

"Healthy and employed, I'll settle for that." Stanforth rose from the chair and stood swaying for a moment. "I'm off. And I believe I should walk."

Indy approached him. "Thanks for taking the stand you did. I won't forget."

Stanforth showed him a woozy look. "Yes, I cut quite the dramatic figure, don't I? The members of the board were stunned into shamed silence. At least that's the way I'll tell it to the grandkids." He zigzagged to the front door, turning around when he reached it. "When you're young you spend all your time thinking: 'Who will I be?' And in the end you find yourself shouting at the world, 'This is who I am.'"

At the closet, Indy regarded his fedora and coiled

bullwhip in silence. *My secret identity?* he wondered. Or were the tweed suit, bifocals, and mild-mannered personality just a costume?

Behind him, Stanforth went on. "But lately I've been asking myself, after I'm gone who will people say I was?"

Indeed, Indy thought, leaving the hat and whip where they were and closing the closet.

CHAPTER EIGHT

*T*he college town's train station consisted of a small parking lot, a charming fieldstone building that contained a ticket booth and waiting room, and tin-roofed concrete platforms on either side of the tracks. The Hartford–New Haven train to New York City's Grand Central Station had already pulled in and was announcing imminent departure with long blasts of its whistle.

In the parking area, Indy climbed from the backseat of a taxi. Suitcase in hand, he hurried up the baggage ramp that accessed the westbound platform, straightening his jacket and tie as he ran.

He viewed his last-minute arrival as a sign of his ongoing ambivalence about leaving. For most of the night he had tossed and turned, grappling with the gravity of his decision and thinking through the events in Nevada and wondering about the current whereabouts of Mac, Spalko, and Dovchenko. Assuming the Russians were still in the States, shouldn't he be out hunting for them? Or was an adventure of that nature better left to the FBI, and younger men in general?

For at least an hour Indy had been certain he was better off remaining in the States, if only to clear his name — even if that meant appearing before some Congressional or intelligence oversight committee. But by four A.M. he had changed his mind. Without his professorship, there was nothing to keep him in Connecticut or anywhere else. And perhaps he really was getting too old for fortune and glory — for adventuring of the sort Marcus Brody had financed up until his death in '52, first as curator of the National Museum, then as dean of students at Marshall College.

Edging through the crowd of commuters on the platform, Indy pulled himself onto the diamond-plate forward stairs of one of the cars. Had he not been so sleep deprived, he might have taken note of a pair of burly men in dark suits who boarded the same car by its rear stairs.

The whistle blew once more and the train jolted into forward motion. Indy was about to enter the car's vestibule when he heard the roar of a motorcycle engine, and turned to see a young man planted atop a modified Harley-Davidson zoom up the baggage ramp and begin to slalom through the crowd of suddenly alarmed passengers and furious redcaps, as if intent on giving chase to the departing train.

The motorcycle rider was dressed in a fashion that had recently been popularized by actors like Marlon Brando, James Dean, Elvis Presley, and other wild ones and rebels: leather jacket, leather gloves, cuffed dungarees, black boots, wraparound sunglasses, and long hair so filled with hair wax that the kid's pompadour wasn't even moving in the wind.

As the motorcycle came even with the passenger car, Indy was surprised to hear the kid yell: "Hey, mister! Hey, buddy! Hey, professor!"

Indy didn't recognize the kid as one of his students. He took a moment to glance up the tracks, to the stone wall of an overpass tunnel the train was about to enter. "You're running out of platform, kid. If you have something to say, you'd better make it fast." To emphasize the point, he turned and began to ascend into the vestibule.

The kid whipped off his sunglasses, steering the bike with one hand. "You're an old friend of Harold Oxley, right?"

Indy stopped short and whirled. "What about him?"

"They're gonna kill him!" the kid said as he applied the brakes.

The train disappeared into the tunnel, and for a moment, it appeared to have taken Indy with it. But in fact

Indy was standing amid the crowd, just short of the stone wall, the suitcase dangling from his hand.

And not far behind were the two men who were shadowing him.

Most Saturdays, Arnie's Diner was packed with a mixed crowd of Marshall College undergrads, high school lettermen, poodle-skirted teenage girls, and townies sporting leather jackets and ducktail haircuts. With a football game under way in the stadium and a protest march making its way down Main Street, Arnie's was even more packed than usual. Still, Indy and the biker had managed to score a table, close to where a gaggle of girls in saddle shoes was gathered at the jukebox and a gang of young toughs was looking for trouble.

Indy was staring at a photograph of the Harley rider, showing him standing alongside a conservatively dressed, studious-looking man in his early fifties.

"Ox and I haven't spoken in twenty years," Indy said, "but I recognize even this version of him."

"Why'd you two stop talking?" the kid asked from the bench seat opposite Indy's.

Indy stroked his jaw. "I'm not sure. He cut me off, angry about something. He never told me why. But I miss him. He was a brilliant guy. Even if he could talk you to sleep once he got going on a topic."

The biker grinned in recollection. "When I was a kid, that's exactly how I got to sleep. The Ox was better than warm milk." He extended his hand across the table. "I'm Mutt. Mutt Williams."

Indy raised an eyebrow. "Mutt? What kind of name is that?"

Mutt's face took on sudden color. "The one I picked. You have a problem with it?"

Indy leaned back in his chair. After all America had fought so hard to achieve in World War II, here was this twenty-year-old kid, the very picture of his spoiled generation, raised on television and frozen meals and consumer fads, and yet so filled with anger it practically oozed out of him.

"Take it easy," Indy said at last. He returned the photograph. "Are you related to Ox?"

"I always thought of him as my uncle, even though he isn't." Mutt paused. "My dad died in the war, and the Ox kind of helped my mom raise me."

Pulling a pocket comb from his dungarees, Mutt ran it through his carefully kept hair. Indy followed his gaze to an athletic boy in a letter sweater, one arm draped over the shoulders of a ponytailed girl.

Indy glanced at his watch. "Kid, the last train leaves in thirty minutes, so if you've got a story to tell, now's the time."

Clearly, Mutt didn't like being told what to do, but he bit back whatever he had in mind to say and started again. "Six months ago my mom got a letter from the Ox. It was mailed from Peru. Ox wrote that he'd found some kind of crystal skull. You know, like the one that guy Mitchell-Hedges found." Pivoting in the seat, he snatched a bottle from a tray in the hands of a passing waitress.

"How do you know about the Mitchell-Hedges skull?" With equal aplomb, Indy snatched the bottle from Mutt and replaced it on the tray.

Mutt frowned, then laughed shortly. "Ox could talk about that thing till the cows came home. What was it, like an idol?"

Indy nodded. "It's a deity carving. There's a few crystal skulls around the world. I saw one at an expo at the British Museum."

"Ox said that the skull has psychic powers."

"Stare into the eyes of the skull and learn the secrets of the universe," Indy said, "or maybe go mad." He smiled in a patronizing way. "Impressively crafted, but that's about it."

"Oh yeah?" Mutt said. "Well, laugh all you want to, but Ox said he found one in Peru, and that this one was *real* different. He said he was bringing it to a place called Akator."

Indy leaned forward in sudden interest. "Akator? Are you sure?"

"Yeah. Why? What is it?"

Reflexively, Indy lowered his voice. "If you believe the stories, it's a lost city in the Amazon. The one the conquistadors called El Dorado."

Mutt nodded. "I've heard of El Dorado."

"The way it goes, seven thousand years ago a native tribe called the Ugha was tasked by its gods to construct a city of solid gold. With the help of the gods, the tribe raised the city and invented technology that was thousands of years ahead of its time. In 1546, a conquistador named Francesco de Orellana — he was known as the Gilded Man, because of his love of gold — disappeared into the Amazon looking for Akator. In the 1920's, a British explorer named Percy Fawcett also disappeared. I've even looked for it. Almost died of typhus on one expedition."

"*You* looked for it?" Mutt said with a laugh. "That sounds like another legend."

Indy let the remark go and sat back into his chair. "You're confusing me with Akator."

"Okay. So even if Akator doesn't exist, why would Ox want to take the crystal skull there?"

"Because there's more to the story. Some say that a

crystal skull was stolen from Akator in the fifteenth or six-teenth century, precisely when Orellana and others were looking for the place. It's believed in parts of South America that whoever finds the missing skull and returns it to Akator's temple will be granted control over its power."

Indy fell silent for a moment. One heard such tales recounted late at night in dark cantinas or flea-ridden jungle flophouses, whispered by elderly men in tattered clothing who had gone too many days without sleep or had downed too much *aguardiente*.

"Power? What kind of power?" Mutt asked.

"I don't know, kid," Indy said, coming back to himself. "It's just a *story*." He looked at Mutt. "Is that the end of yours?"

Mutt shook his head. "Judging by the letter, my mom thought the Ox was going crazy." He tapped his forefinger against his head. "Smog in the noggin. So she went down to Peru hoping to find him. Instead she learned that somebody had kidnapped him, and once she got on the kidnappers' trail they nabbed her, too. The kidnappers claim that Ox hid the crystal skull someplace, and that if my mom can't talk him into revealing the hiding place or find it herself, one of them's gonna die." He looked hard at Indy. "She said you'd help."

"Me? How does your mom know me? What's her name?"

"Mary Williams. You remember her?"

Indy smiled. "There've been a lot of Mary Williams in my life, kid."

"Hey, shut up, man. This is my mom we're talking about."

Indy waved his hands in a placating gesture. "Simmer down. Look, you don't have to get sore all the time just to show everybody how tough you are, okay?"

Somewhat appeased, Mutt said, "My mom said if anybody could find the skull, it's you. You're some kind of grave robber or something, right?"

"Grave — I'm a *teacher*." Indy let it hang in the air; then added: "How do you know she's been kidnapped?"

"She called me two weeks ago from South America. She'd escaped, but they were after her. She said she'd mailed me a letter the Ox had written when the kidnappers were holding both of them, and that I should get it to you. Then the phone line went dead."

Mutt reached into one of the black jacket's zippered pockets and produced a stained envelope. Opening the envelope's flap, Indy pulled out a folded sheet of paper.

"It's complete gibberish," Mutt said. "Ain't even in English lettering."

Indy was about to reply when his gaze fell on two dark-suited goons seated on stools at the soda fountain. Mutt looked at him questioningly.

"What —"

"Those two bricks at the soda counter," Indy said quietly. "They're not here for the milk shakes."

"Who are they?"

"I don't know. FBI, maybe."

He had no sooner uttered the words when the men slid from the stools and began to make their way to the table. Quickly, Indy stashed the letter in his jacket pocket.

"Come quietly, Dr. Jones," the first goon to reach the table said in Russian-accented English. "And be sure to bring the letter with you."

"Make that KGB," Indy said to Mutt. To the Russians, he said, "What letter?"

"The letter Mr. Williams just gave you," the second Russian said.

Mutt gestured to himself. "Me? Do I *look* like a mailman?"

The Russians didn't so much as crack a smile. "We don't ask again," the same one said. "Come now or —"

"Or what?" Mutt broke in.

Indy heard a loud *click!* and saw that Mutt's folded arms concealed a stiletto, its long blade reflecting the light of the blinking jukebox. At the same time, Indy saw the

Russian's hand go to the waistband of his trousers. The barrel of a .45 peeked from inside the Russian's suit jacket, aimed at the side of Indy's head.

"Nice try, kid," Indy told Mutt. "But you brought a knife to a gunfight."

CHAPTER NINE

On your feet. Outside," the first Russian said, as if he had grown up watching gangster movies.

The second Russian relieved Mutt of the knife, retracting the blade and slipping it into his jacket pocket. "Now!" he whispered, when Indy and Mutt didn't move quickly enough.

As Indy had learned in Nevada, Irina Spalko's secret agents were deadly serious about getting their way. He berated himself for having lowered his guard. In the old days he would have been glancing over his shoulder at every turn, but he had dropped the habit after the war, resigning from the OSS after what was left of the organization had been reborn as the Central Intelligence Agency. Besides, like many Americans, he had become more concerned about being "of interest" to the FBI than about being shadowed by Soviet operatives, Cold War or no.

Briefly he considered calling for help or yelling "Fire!" but this wasn't Doom Town. He feared that the Russians would simply start shooting, and innocent people would end up getting hurt. It was bad enough that he now had Mutt Williams to worry about. He could already imagine the Russians holding pistols to the kid's head, threatening to kill him unless Indy did what they demanded. In this case, that would involve handing over the cryptic letter Harold Oxley had allegedly written, or maybe translating it.

The pieces of Spalko's plot were beginning to fall into place, but this wasn't the time or place to think through it. He had to come up with some means for Mutt to escape. That way, at least, the Russians wouldn't have a hostage to use in forcing Indy's hand.

At Indy's nod, he and Mutt slid from the booth and fell in between the two brawny agents, whose right hands were wedged with clear purpose into the pockets of their dark suit jackets. As they maneuvered through the crowd of teens and frat boys, two more Russians entered Arnie's through the front door. Indy's eyes darted from the door to the soda fountain to the blaring jukebox. A few more steps and Mutt would be edging past a college letterman who was chatting up a girl wearing a poodle skirt. Again, Indy's eyes darted, this time from the varsity sports letter on the kid's sweater to Mutt's black leather jacket and to the huddle of young hoodlums laughing it up at a nearby table.

"Mutt," Indy said out of the side of his mouth, "punch the prep in the face."

Mutt turned slightly in Indy's direction. "Huh?"

"Joe College," Indy said, gesturing with his chin and transferring his suitcase to his left hand. "Give him a knuckle sandwich. Don't break his jaw, but give him a good tap."

Following Indy's gaze to the letterman, Mutt grinned. "With pleasure." To make things easier, he veered left as he walked; then, when he and the college kid were practically shoulder to shoulder, he whirled, saying, "Hey, nosebleed."

Poor Joe College turned, and Mutt's balled-up fist caught him right on the side of the jaw, dropping him to the floor. The girl in the poodle skirt screamed, and shouts of outrage rang out from all sides.

"Get that greaser!" another letterman railed.

Quick to deduce Indy's plan, the two Russian escorts tried to grab hold of Mutt and Indy and hustle them out the front door. But three of the letterman's varsity teammates had already pounced on Mutt, and Indy had sidestepped out of reach into a press of kids who were eager to join the fray.

Seeing one of their own being set upon, the townies at the table sprang from their seats, muscling their way to Mutt's aid with kicks and swinging fists. A hurled chair landed on the Formica table of one of the booths, initiating a separate fight between two kids in khaki and three hoods in denim. As the mayhem continued to mount, someone slammed into the jukebox. A needle scratched across vinyl and the teen yearnings of "The Glory of Love" were suddenly replaced by the boogie-woogie beat of Bill Haley's rendition of "Shake, Rattle and Roll."

Ducking down, Indy yanked two of the lettermen off Mutt's back, punched the third one in the face, and nailed one of the hoods while he was at it. Mutt flashed him a grin and came to his feet swinging, his fist connecting with one of the Russian agents, who thudded to the floor.

"C'mon!" Indy said.

Hurling his suitcase at the Russians, he began to shoulder his way to the front door. Mutt bent down to fish his switchblade from the agent's jacket pocket and followed. Behind them, chaos held their would-be captors in check. The pair who had entered the diner moments earlier could do little more than shout for them to stop, in Russian and in English.

Bursting out the front door, Indy and Mutt raced into the side alley where Mutt had parked the motorcycle.

Ignition key in hand, Mutt straddled the seat, gave a twist to the key, and stomped on the starter. Granted a moment to think, Indy allowed his thoughts to unfurl.

In her quest for objects of paranormal power, Irina Spalko had learned that a crystal skull had been unearthed in Peru. She had tracked down and ultimately captured Oxley, but by then he had already hidden the skull. Employing a different strategy, Spalko had allowed Oxley to pass a secret message to Mutt Williams' mother, certain that the message would eventually reach Indy.

"Your mom didn't escape, kid," he told Mutt over the sudden roar of the bike. "They let her go. They wanted her to mail Ox's letter, and they wanted you to bring that letter to me. Now they want me to translate it, and they plan on using you to make me do it."

"Not likely," Mutt said. Toeing the bike into gear, he motioned to the rear fender, which was flanked by saddlebags. "Get on, Clyde. Time to cut out!"

Indy threw one leg over the rear wheel and sat down as best he could. "You sure you're old enough to handle this thing in a chase?"

Mutt twisted the throttle and looked over his shoulder. "The question you should be asking yourself is whether you're young enough to hang on."

Just then a black sedan skidded to a stop at the entrance to the alley.

Mutt popped the clutch and the motorcycle shot forward, its front wheel a couple of inches off the ground. He aimed straight for the Russians emerging from the car, who threw themselves to either side. Indy leaned his body to the right, his fingers searching for handholds, as Mutt laid into a lightning-fast turn and bolted down the street.

Zigzagging through traffic, Mutt climbed through the gears, the hog's powerful engine growling in delight. But they hadn't gone more than a couple of blocks when a second sedan leaped out at them from a side street, then screeched into a fishtailing turn in pursuit. Drivers palmed their horns and shouted curses from the windows, but the Russians paid them no heed. Tires squealing, the sedan accelerated sharply, catching up with Mutt, then coming alongside him on the inside, intent on forcing the motorcycle into oncoming traffic.

Mutt evaded the sedan for a moment, but soon found himself trapped between the sedan on the left and a bus in the adjacent lane. With what struck Indy as deliberate cruelty, the Russian driver veered the sedan ever so slowly to the right, forcing Mutt to swerve until he and Indy were in danger of being crushed against the side of the bus.

But Indy had apparently been wrong about Mutt's importance to Spalko's latest ploy, because two pairs of arms suddenly reached through the sedan's rear passenger-side window and dragged Indy completely off the bike.

Completely off the bike and directly into the rear seat.

Anything but an obliging passenger, Indy jabbed one of the Russians in the nose and began to crawl over the lap of the second one, determined to escape through the lowered driver's-side window.

Through the rear window of the sedan he saw that Mutt had extricated himself from the Russian driver's squeeze play and had decelerated to fall behind the sedan. Now, gunning the Harley, Mutt jinked to his left and came up even with the sedan on that side. By then, Indy had his hands gripped on the window frame and was squirming in the grip of the Russian who wasn't holding his bleeding nose. Contorting his body into a fetal position, he kicked out with both feet, smashing his opponent squarely in the face. As a consequence, though, he wound up propelling himself halfway through the window, his arms flailing for purchase and his face only inches from the pavement.

Seeing Indy's predicament, Mutt angled the bike closer to the sedan. When the bike was within reach, Indy fastened his hands on the frame and heaved himself fully out the window, though more forcefully than he had planned. Failing to nail the perfect landing he had in mind, Indy found himself clinging to the back of the bike like a water-skier on dry land, arms threatening to come loose from their sockets and shoes burning up on the pavement.

Realizing that Indy had overshot the bike, Mutt tapped the brakes hard, but only long enough to allow Indy's forward momentum to carry him up over the rear fender, slamming into Mutt's leather-clad back, and down on the fender, where he belonged. Up ahead, however, another sedan had entered the chase, darting from a side street to head off the bike. Mutt slewed to the right at the last second, but not into a side street or alley. Instead, the motorcycle began bounding up the broad steps of the town library. In no time flat it was inside the building, sending students scurrying for cover, and books, magazines, and periodicals sailing into the air. Judging by his gleeful laugh, Mutt was obviously enjoying himself immensely. So much so, Indy thought, that — as at the train station — he had somehow failed to notice the wall that was looming up in front of them.

"Mutt!" Indy shouted into his ear.

Mutt gave the hog's handlebars a violent tug, but the rear tire was no match for the library's polished hardwood floor, and the bike went down on its side, barreling through the reading room like a bulldozer and sending Indy and Mutt sprawling.

Plainly a veteran of intentional ditches, Mutt was back on his feet in a flash, righting the bike and slamming his foot down on the starter.

Slower to rise and furious, Indy yelled, "I'm driving!"

But Mutt only looked at him and laughed. "Fat chance." When the engine roared back to life, he whipped his comb out and began to restore his pompadour.

Clearing his head with a shake, Indy was dusting himself off when two students from one of his archaeology classes approached him cautiously.

"Uh, Dr. Jones," the shorter of the two said. "Just got a quick question about Hargrove's normative culture models . . ."

"Forget Hargrove," Indy said, still clapping dust from his jacket. "Read Vere Gorden Childe on diffusionism. He spent most of his life in the field." He climbed aboard the bike, and Mutt revved the engine. "If you want to be a good archaeologist . . ." he added as Mutt toed the bike into gear and shot for the building's rear doors, ". . . you've got to get out of the library!"

Barging through the doors, Indy and Mutt bounced down onto a heavily trafficked street that led to the center of town. Indy thought that they might have given their pursuers the slip until he spied one of the Russians' sedans speed into view. Mutt saw the car as well and pulled a fast U-turn, shooting for the town square. Cars were backed up for blocks, but Mutt wove through them effortlessly. Two blocks from the square, however, the way was blocked by a group of marchers waving placards, holding banners aloft, and chanting slogans. Mutt hesitated for a moment, then took the bike right into the march.

Indy was sure that they had lost the Russians, but he was wrong again. The same sedan had made use of the sidewalk to circumvent the traffic backup and was now pursuing them into the heart of the demonstration.

Mutt accelerated, coming dangerously close to running over some of the demonstrators, but at the same time increasing their lead on the sedan.

Leaning on the horn, the Russian driver tried to scatter the marchers, but they weren't having any of it. Not until the sedan lunged forward with intent, leaving rubber on the road behind it and forcing the crowd to part. Indy saw a placard go airborne as a protestor dove to one side, its slogan visible for the instant before it slapped down on the sedan's windshield.

Better dead than Red.

On the far side of the town square stood the college football stadium, a brick structure with broad entrance ramps leading to various seating areas.

Mutt was angling the bike onto a street that ran west of the stadium when he changed his mind. Leaning low to the pavement, he threw the bike into a sudden turn, hurtling onto one of the access ramps and straight onto the playing field, where a game was in progress!

Seeing the Harley, the roar of the crowd went from

enthusiastic to indignant, but that didn't stop Mutt. On the thirty-yard line, a quarterback had just received the hike and was dropping back to hurl a pass, even as a cluster of defensive linesmen was rushing him. When the rushers began angling for the sidelines, the quarterback whirled through a half circle to find a motorcycle streaking straight at him down the center of the field, Mutt leaning over the handlebars, Indy holding on for all it was worth.

Worse still, the motorcycle riders were being chased by a sedan that had come plowing through a wooden fence at the end of the field, and was now churning up the gridiron in an effort to narrow the bike's lead.

Quick on his feet, the quarterback managed to dodge both the motorcycle and the sedan, and uncertain as to just what rules or penalties might apply to the presence of vehicles on the field, he let fly a long arcing pass, in the hope that one of his teammates would catch it.

Mutt, meanwhile, had already zipped through the line of scrimmage and was now zigzagging the bike downfield, through players on both teams, the sedan gaining ground as the Harley neared the end zone. Glancing over his shoulder, Indy saw the football in ballistic free fall just over his head. Instinctively, he reached his arms out, and the pigskin landed squarely in his hands as the Harley shot between the goalposts.

The crowd came to its feet, and Indy, turning once more, sent the football spiraling straight at the head of the sedan's driver. Together, the motorcycle and the car dashed across the end zone and disappeared into a sloping, tile-walled exit tunnel. Somehow Mutt managed to keep the bike upright as it bounced and bounded onto the road, ringing the stadium, but, slumped over the steering wheel, the driver of the sedan didn't fare nearly as well.

Wavering from its course, the sedan crashed head-on into a plinth of white granite, atop which sat a bronze statue of a smiling Marcus Brody, whose head and shoulders toppled through the windshield to rest squarely between the two unconscious Russian agents.

CHAPTER TEN

*H*ours later, the streets dark and deserted, Indy directed Mutt to his cottage on the campus. Concealing the motorcycle behind a tall hedge, they observed the house for several minutes before entering it — at a rush.

Mutt took in the comfortable furnishings, the small piano and large world globe. "Who lives here?" he asked while Indy was making straight for the small den.

"I do."

"You?!" Mutt said, following him. "This'll be the first place they look for us!"

"Which doesn't give us much time." Indy was standing at a built-in bookcase, his head tilted to one side to scan the titles of the closely packed volumes.

"Time for what?"

Indy ignored the question. Oxley's letter in hand, he was comparing the enigmatic symbols to those on the page of a thick book he had pulled from the case. "I thought so," he said at last. "Koihoma."

"Coy-what?"

"An obscure pre-Columbian language," he said without lifting his eyes from the page. "Precursor to Olmec, Mayan, and Nahuatl, some say." Extending the letter to Mutt, he added: "See these symbols? They're glyphs — rudimentary glyphs, but glyphs just the same. Mayan syllabary system, combining pictographs and ideograms." He nodded, grinning. "Ox, you clever devil. Anagrams, acrostics, puns . . ."

Mutt's brow furrowed. "You speak Coy . . . whatever you said?"

Indy glanced at him. "Speak it? Ha! No one does, and maybe no one ever did. It may have only been a written form of the lingua franca."

"The lin —"

Indy flipped pages in the book. "But I can decipher it — some of it, anyway. Just have to run it through Landa's Mayan alphabet first."

"You some kind of language expert?"

"*Linguist* is the term you're searching for. But, yeah, I am."

"How many do you speak?"

"I don't know," Indy said in a distracted way. "Two dozen or so. More if you include hieroglyphs and such."

Mutt's jaw dropped. "Two dozen? I can barely get by in Spanish."

"Or English, from the sound of it," Indy muttered. Having trouble focusing on the text in the book, he reached into his jacket pocket for his wire-rim bifocals, clearing his throat in a self-conscious way as he hooked the arms of the glasses around his ears. Grabbing a pad from the table, he began to scribble notes on the top sheet.

Mutt watched him for a moment. "You know, for an old guy, you ain't bad in a fight."

"Thanks a bunch, kid," Indy said.

Mutt smiled lightly. "So what are you, like eighty?"

Indy laughed in a resigned way. "Not yet. But what you see's the result of hard living. Can't say I recommend it." Turning, he showed Mutt the notes he had written. "Partial transcription of Ox's letter. He wrote: 'Follow the lines in the earth only gods can read to Orellana's cradle, guarded by the living dead.'"

"Orellana," Mutt said. "The gilded conquistador, right?"

Indy nodded. "You catch on fast. But . . . 'only gods can read . . .' What could Ox —" He stopped himself and smiled. "Of course! He means the Nazca Lines."

Leaping to his feet, Indy climbed a moveable ladder affixed to the bookcase and pulled a volume from one of the upper shelves. Hopping down to the floor, he flipped through the book, then set it in front of Mutt. Spanning two pages were aerial photographs of a stylized spider, a hummingbird, a curly-tailed monkey, a lizard, and a large-headed humanoid figure.

"Geoglyphs," Indy explained. "More or less etched into the desert floor in that part of Peru. Some were done as early as two hundred B.C. But the thing of it is, they can only be seen from the air." He looked at Mutt. "You get it? Only gods can read them because the gods reside in the sky."

Mutt blinked. "Is all this gonna be on the test? 'Cause I —"

"Oxley's telling us that the crystal skull is somewhere in Nazca, Peru."

"I still don't get why Russians want the thing so badly."

"The Kremlin must think the skull is some kind of weapon. Like Ox, they're convinced that the skull has psychic power. But that power is given only to the person who returns the skull to the lost city of Akator."

"Power or not, if giving the skull to them means that my mom and Oxley can go free, then I'm all for finding it." Shooting to his feet, Mutt added: "Just try not to slow me down."

Turning to a different page, Indy ran his finger down

the text, reading in a low voice. On the facing page was a seemingly fanciful illustration of Akator, set at the summit of a flat-topped mesa and encircled by thick forest.

"The Inca claimed that Akator was located at the Fourth Corner of Twantinsuyu — their word for their empire, the known world." Mostly to himself, he said, "Akator would be the find of a lifetime. Even politicians would steer clear of going after someone who finds Akator."

Reaching for the first book he had taken from the bookcase, he tore out several symbol-filled pages and crammed them into his jacket pocket. Then, while Mutt hurried out the front door, he made straight for the bedroom closet, where his fedora and bullwhip were just where he had left them. Planting the hat on his head, he gave the leather-covered handle of the bullwhip a strong tug, forcing it to uncoil from the closet pole with a loud *crack!*

Peru is only a few degrees of longitude east of New York City, but planes seldom fly in straight lines, and the world turns under our feet.

At LaGuardia International, Indy and Mutt — along with Mutt's motorcycle — boarded a plane for Mexico City. There, after killing an afternoon visiting the fabled ruins of Teotihuacán, they transferred to a smaller plane, which touched down for refueling in Panama City and Quito, Ecuador, on its way to Lima, Peru.

In that coastal capital city of cool mist and conspicuous danger, the new partners explored their options for continuing south by land, sea, or air. Ultimately, Indy found space for them aboard a cargo plane destined for the Peruvian city of Arequipa. The pilot had agreed — for a fistful of dollars — to alight briefly at Nazca's small desert airstrip.

On the approach to Nazca, the pilot, as a bonus, swung his craft in a broad circle above the Pampas de Jumana to treat his American passengers to a view of the famous lines that for two millennia could be read only by the gods.

CHAPTER ELEVEN

*M*utt had gotten himself into tight spots before, but never as tight as this one. Stuck in the armpit of Peru with a crazy old coot adventurer who, when he wasn't telling stories about the glory days, was lecturing Mutt about Incan ruins and the tragic history of South America. If any of this was getting them one step closer to finding his mom or Oxley or locating the supposedly hidden crystal skull, then maybe Mutt might have gone along with it. But as it was, he and Jones just seemed to be waving off flies in furnace-hot Nazca.

Mutt had seen a lot of places in Europe, but Peru was a whole new world. The desert town was a baked grid of squat, whitewashed buildings with terra-cotta tile roofs. Seedy cantinas outnumbered the town's moldering churches by about ten to one, and stray dogs outnumbered the cantinas. Armed desperados with dark, drooping mustachios rubbed shoulders with wiry *campesinos* in filthy clothes, sporting razor-sharp machetes on their hips.

Rummage around in the dark shops and you might be able to find tins of sardines and tomato sauce, but elsewhere the menu consisted of rice, beans, and usually unidentifiable hunks of scrawny chicken. The previous night, Mutt had watched a rooster claw bob to the surface of the thick soup a waiter had set before him. By day, the small market area teemed with Andean highlanders, descendants of the Inca, wearing striped ponchos, sandals made from hemp or the rubber from old car tires, and fedoras or woolen ear-flapped caps, bartering for potatoes of every conceivable color, shape, and size, or ears of corn more fit for cattle than humans. And at night, on the street corners, vendors would sell chunks of grilled beef heart or guinea pigs run through by thin wooden skewers, or tall glasses of a home-brewed beer the indigenous people called *chicha*.

The first couple of days in Nazca, Mutt had taken the motorcycle for rides on the pampa, opening the bike up in a way he rarely got to do in the States. But it wasn't long before dust and sand sabotaged the fun, and he was forced to spend more time cleaning the carburetor than joyriding.

The only vegetation to be found was in Nazca's small

central square, where a couple of aged eucalyptus trees provided shade. Mutt had made a habit of killing the afternoon hours at a restaurant on the plaza's north side, where he could chain the bike to an old iron lamppost and nurse sodas while Jones pressed the locals for information that might lead them to Oxley, Mary, or their captors.

Mutt was into his fifth soda of the afternoon, and all that sugar was starting to make him feel antsy. When he placed the bottle at the crown on a pyramid of other bottles, he noticed that his hand was shaking.

Just then Jones came around the corner, laughing it up with a couple of highlanders. He thanked them and hurried over to join Mutt at the table.

"Finally," Indy began. "They say they remember Ox. A couple of months back he came staggering into town, ranting like a wild man."

"No shortage of madmen in Nazca," Mutt chimed in.

"True enough. But foreigners are treated differently. When none of the local *medicos* or *curanderos* were able to calm him down, the police had no choice but to bring him to the sanitarium."

Mutt snorted. "Figures there'd be a loony bin here."

Indy stood up. "It's at the south edge of town. We can walk or take your bike. What do you want to do?"

Mutt glanced at the Harley. "Will it be safe?"

Indy considered it. "Probably safer here than it would be at the sanitarium."

"Okay, then. We walk."

Indy set out a brisk pace, Mutt hurrying to fall into step beside him. "What language were those highlanders speaking? Sure wasn't Spanish."

"Quechua," Indy said. "It was the traders' tongue of the Inca Empire. Now it's the first language of the mountain people."

"So you learned it here in Peru?"

Indy laughed at some personal recollection. "Actually, I learned it in Mexico."

"Quechua's spoken that far north?"

"No, it isn't. But, well . . . it's a long story."

"So what? Maybe you haven't noticed, but we've got nothing but time."

Indy nodded. "I learned Quechua from a Peruvian who rode with Pancho Villa." He glanced at Mutt while they walked. "I was with Villa's army for a short time."

"No way," Mutt said.

"I didn't enlist. Technically, I was kidnapped into the army."

Mutt did the math in his head. "But you couldn't've even been twenty years old."

"You're right."

"Your parents must have had a cow. Did they have to pay a ransom to get you back?"

"Things were . . ." Indy said, laughing again, "a little tense at home. But it all worked out in the end."

Mutt fell silent for a moment. "My mom and I weren't on the best of terms when she came down here looking for Ox."

Indy nodded in sympathy. "Treat her right, kid. You only get one, and sometimes not for very long."

Mutt frowned. "Maybe so, but it ain't my problem, it's hers. She got p.o.-ed 'cause I quit school, like some goof or something."

"High school?"

"More than one. And lots of fancy prep schools, too."

"Why's that?"

Mutt made a gesture of dismissal. "All they do is teach you chess, debate, fencing." He glanced at Indy. "I can handle a blade like nobody's business. But what a waste of time. And they make you study the wrong stuff. I mean, I like books — Ox made me read everything under the sun when I was a kid — but now at least I get to pick the ones I want to read, you know what I mean?"

Indy returned a tentative nod. "So, instead of attending school you work."

"When I can, yeah."

"Doing what?"

"Mechanic work. Mostly repairing motorcycles." He glanced at Indy. "Bikes are getting more and more popular. When I get good enough with my hands, I'll have it made in the shade."

"Plan on doing that forever?"

Mutt shot him another look. "Maybe I do, man. Anything wrong with that?"

Indy smiled. "Not a thing, kid. And don't let anybody tell you different." He stopped suddenly and pivoted on his heel, eyeing the storefronts and several locals who were about.

"What is it?" Mutt asked.

Indy continued. "Probably nothing. Just felt like someone was watching us a little too closely."

CHAPTER TWELVE

*T*he sanitarium occupied part of a centuries-old monastery that stood on its own at the edge of town. Indy gazed up at the stone-and-adobe façade to read the words that were carved in wood above the building's hulking doors.

"Saint Anthony de Padua," he said, smirking. "The patron saint of lost things."

A nun wearing a kind of winged hat answered their knocks and admitted them.

"We're looking for an American named Harold Oxley," Indy explained in Spanish.

The nun thought for a moment. "I remember him. He was here a couple of months ago, but men came and stole him away." She paused, then added in a whisper, "Men with guns."

"Men with guns," Indy said, translating and glancing knowingly at Mutt. "Sister, could you perhaps show us to the room where he was confined?"

"*Por supuesto, caballero. Por aquí.*"

Mutt and Indy followed her inside and down a long, dank corridor festooned with cobwebs. Diffuse, dust-laden light streamed through plate-glass panels set high in the round-arched ceiling. In a tall niche stood a wooden statue of St. Anthony fronted by iron racks of squat votive candles. And from somewhere, a warped recording of classical music was playing on an old gramophone.

A short distance along, Mutt began to lag behind, his gaze jumping nervously to the murky cells that lined both sides of the hallway. Behind barred windows in the thick doors he caught glimpses of men and women dressed in tatters, mumbling to themselves or their fellow cellmates, crying, shrieking, laughing maniacally, or huddled silently in the dark recesses.

"*Hola, señor,*" said a male inmate standing at the window of one of the cells. "*Venga, señor,*" he added, beckoning to Mutt with crooked, sallow fingers. "Come here, come here."

Mutt suddenly felt like he had walked out of a Western into an old horror movie replete with ghosts, ghouls, madmen, and monsters. He approached the cell of the inmate who had called out to him. Not that he could understand a word of the man's rapid and incessant ramblings.

"*No comprendo,*" Mutt said, wondering for a moment

whether the inmate was speaking in tongues. "I don't understand a word —"

Without warning, the inmate lunged forward, grabbing Mutt by the collar of his motorcycle jacket and pulling him against the iron bars. At the same time, three of the man's cellmates hurried forward to paw at Mutt. Swallowing hard to find his voice, Mutt had just begun to stammer a cry for help when another pair of hands clamped hold of him from behind, yanking him free of the inmates' hold and whirling him around.

"Try to keep up," Indy said matter-of-factly as Mutt rushed to rejoin him and the nun.

"Sister María says that Oxley was deranged when he was brought here," Indy went on. "Obsessed and sometimes hysterical. He drew pictures all over the walls of his cell."

Mutt heard a squeaking sound issuing from somewhere in front of them and saw a crippled old janitor appear out of the gloom, pushing a wheeled cart. When he returned his gaze to Indy, Indy had Oxley's letter in hand and was squinting at it.

"'The lines only the gods can read,'" Indy said. "Okay, that much we know. But Ox goes on to write, 'leading to Orellana's cradle.'" He gave his head a shake. "It doesn't make sense. Francisco de Orellana wasn't born in Peru. He arrived here with Pizarro and was the first

European to navigate the length of the Amazon River before he returned to the jungle to search for El Dorado. He and his six lieutenants were never heard from again. So how could the Nazca Lines, any of them, lead to Orellana's 'cradle'?"

Sister María came to a halt in front of one of the cells. Fishing a skeleton key from the pocket of her habit, she inserted it into the lock, then pushed the heavy door wide open and stepped to one side to make room for Indy and Mutt.

The musty-smelling room was approximately twenty feet square, but contained little more than a sagging cloth cot, a stained enamel washbasin, and a wooden bucket. What light there was entered through two small windows on the stone wall opposite the door. When Indy's and Mutt's eyes adjusted to the dark, they saw that the floor was blanketed with inches of windblown sand and that the stone walls were covered floor to ceiling with depictions of human skulls — skulls of every shape and size, and rendered in every style from realistic to abstract. Even the two barred windows had been incorporated as eye sockets into a single enormous drawing.

Mutt's heart sank. "Ox, man, what happened to you?"

Emotion didn't come easy to him, and when he felt Indy's eyes on him, Mutt turned away in embarrassment. When he looked again, Indy was running his fingers over the wall, as if inspecting the words Oxley had scrawled onto them.

"'Return,'" Mutt said, translating one from Spanish.

Indy nodded. "Every word you see written here — in Spanish, Italian, French, even Arabic — means 'return.'"

"Return where?" Mutt said.

"Or return what?" Indy paused. "These drawings don't depict just any old skulls." Using the tip of his forefinger, he traced the outline of the elongated cranium of one of them. Glancing at Mutt, he added, "All of these are depictions of pre-Columbian skulls."

"How do you know that?"

"Pre-Columbian cultures practiced cranial deformation. When an infant was born, its head would be sandwiched between two boards that forced the skull to assume a sloped, elongated shape as the bones knit."

"Why?"

"The jaguar was sacred to many of the ancient cultures. Some experts say that the ancients were attempting to mimic the shape of a jaguar skull." Indy shrugged. "Or maybe it's just a case of beauty being in the eye of the beholder."

Spying something beneath the layer of sand on the floor, Indy found a small hole and began to scoop the sand away with his hand. A moment later, his fingers had

THE HERO

THE VILLAIN

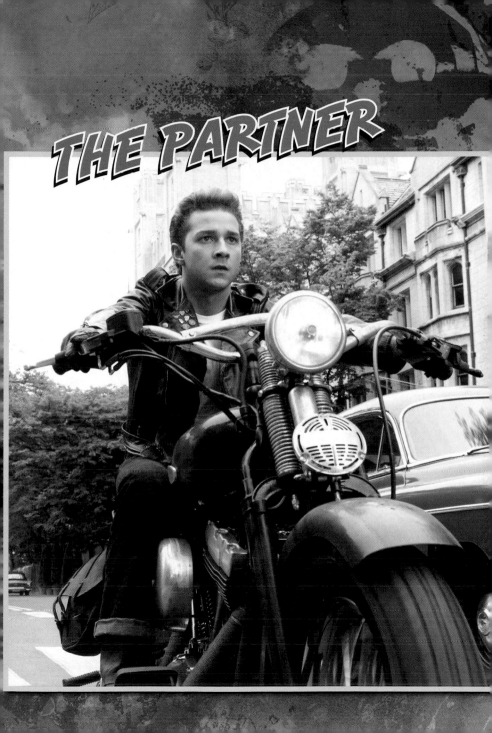

THE STAKES

THE FIGHT

THE PRIZE

discovered a groove of some sort. Peering at the line he had exposed, he said, "Ox etched a drawing into the floor."

Getting to his feet, he rushed out of the cell, only to return an instant later with a broom he had obviously taken from the janitor's cart. "Sweep!" he told Mutt, tossing the broom to him.

Mutt snagged the broom with one hand and went at it, moving the sand into a far corner of the cell. Indy, meanwhile, had found enough hand- and toeholds in the wall to scramble to the ledge of one of the windows, as a means of gazing down on whatever it was Ox had etched into the floor.

Mutt canted his head to one side then the other in an effort to discern what his sweeping had revealed, but he couldn't make heads or tails of the busy etching.

"What is it?" he demanded of Indy. "What did Ox draw?"

"Gravestones," Indy said. "Tombs and crypts and mausoleums, marked with ancient symbols and Christian crosses. Some sort of sacred burial ground."

"A cemetery."

"Exactly."

Mutt lifted his gaze to Indy's perch, ten feet above the floor. "But why would Ox draw a cemetery? What does it mean?"

"It means I was only partially right about the Nazca Lines — the lines only gods can read. *These* are the lines Ox really wanted us to find. And he didn't mean for us to take him literally at his word when he wrote 'cradle.'" Indy showed Mutt a grin. "He was referring to Orellana's resting place — his grave" — he indicated the etching — "in that cemetery."

Mutt mulled it over for a moment. "But didn't you say that Orellana and his bunch had vanished without a trace? That he was never heard from again?"

Indy nodded. "It looks like Oxley found him."

CHAPTER THIRTEEN

Raindrops were as scarce as hen's teeth on the Nazca plateau. Every century or so a storm would blow in from the Pacific Ocean, lashing the area with cold rain and coaxing wildflowers and succulent blooms from the bone-dry landscape. Still, heat lightning was a common occurrence at night in the southern hemisphere's spring, especially in the baked foothills that rose steeply above the desert town.

Bolts fractured the sky as Mutt's Harley switchbacked up an eroded hillside whose summit stuck out like a sore thumb above the Nazca Lines hundreds of feet below. Lizards, chinchillas, and foxes dashed through the beam of the bike's headlamp as Mutt and Indy neared Chauchilla Cemetery at the top, where a flash of brilliant lightning illuminated a sign that read: MATAREMOS A LOS HUAQUEOS!

"We're going to need something to see by," Indy said, climbing off the bike.

Mutt watched him disappear into a caretaker's shack, then switched off the engine and stomped the kickstand into position. After regarding the hand-lettered sign for a moment, he shouted into a gust of wind, "The sign says that grave robbers will be killed."

Just then Indy emerged from the shack, holding a lit lantern in one hand and two shovels in the other, while lightning crackled behind him. "Then it's a good thing we're not grave robbers," he said, grinning.

Mutt followed him through a creaking iron gate. To all sides were vaults and sepulchers, some adorned with wilted flowers or bright bits of crepe paper, others crowned with crosses carved from wood or stone. Some of the tombs were nothing more than engraved marble slabs, where others were mausoleums, larger than the caretaker's shack at the entrance.

Mutt would rather have been anywhere else in the world. "How old is this place?" he asked over Indy's shoulder.

Indy raised the lantern to cast light on one of the tombs. "A thousand years old, at least. Most of the pre-Columbian graves, dating back to the original Nazca culture, were probably looted ages ago." He bent over to peer at numerals inscribed into a slab. "But from the looks of things, the locals have continued using it over the centuries."

"Wouldn't it be easier to bury the bodies down below?" Mutt asked, gulping audibly.

"Easier, yes. But you're not taking local religion into account. The Andean cultures have always been sun and sky worshippers. The closer you could get to the gods, the better. Throughout the Andes you find tombs excavated into the sides and summits of the highest peaks. Because of the arid conditions, bodies mummify naturally. Tombs have been found where the bodies still have hair and nails and the textiles look almost as fresh as the day they were woven."

Mutt was reluctant to take another step, but after a moment he did, trailing Indy as he passed between two gnarled and leafy trees. Had he chanced to look up, he might have noticed the branches of the tree moving, even though the wind had died down. He might even have caught a fleeting glimpse of two shadowy figures materializing from the branches, almost as if they were born of them, and slinking with feline grace into the shadows.

But Mutt's eyes were too riveted on Indy to look anywhere but directly in front of him. Peripherally, he could see that many of the graves had been plundered and despoiled. Yanked from tombs, human skeletons were strewn about, some twisted into impossible postures, and others collapsed into piles of bleached bones. In the flickering flame of the lantern, the flashes of lightning, and the wan light of a rising moon, Mutt could almost imagine that the slack-jawed things were howling at him and Indy for further desecrating their ground.

"I know we're looking for Orellana's grave, but . . . just *what* are we supposed to be looking for?" he asked into a sudden gust of wind.

Indy stopped to look around him. "It won't be any of these aboveground tombs. It'll be underground, or inside a burial mound or barrow. Something that isn't obvious." He handed Mutt one of the shovels. "You'll be needing this."

They began to move deeper into the cemetery. Off to one side, something moved, and Mutt whirled, bringing the shovel up in front of him.

"What now?" Indy said, doubling back.

"I thought I saw something," Mutt explained.

"Ah, you're jumping at shadows. There's nothing here but a bunch of —"

Before Indy could get the rest of it out, something unseen knocked him and Mutt to the ground.

Coming out of nowhere, the blow sent Mutt flying backwards into a lone skeleton propped at the top of the open grave, which immediately came to life and jumped him. Bending sharply at the waist, Mutt catapulted his assailant through a forward somersault, then backed away, feeling along the ground for the shovel. Forked lightning revealed his attacker to be a small, feral-looking human male wearing a mask of facial bones and broad stripes of paint on his chest to suggest ribs. If Mutt had any doubts that his opponent was flesh and blood, they were erased by Indy's fist, which shattered the skeleton mask and sent the man fleeing into the darkness.

"Man, that was *not* dead!" Mutt shouted.

They raised their shovels defensively, and just in time. Two fletched darts flew from the darkness, burying their pointed tips in the wooden handles. By instinct, Indy ducked. Slow to follow, Mutt was suddenly knocked off his feet once more, this time into an open grave filled with recently unearthed corpses. Out of the dark appeared a warrior with a blowgun pressed to his lips. But Mutt was ready for him. Raising his hand, he hurled his opened switchblade straight into the warrior's shoulder. Lurching in pain, the warrior lowered his weapon to clutch at the knife protruding from his flesh. At the same time, a second warrior sprang into action, and Mutt was a sitting duck.

His eyes were fixed on the blowgun when he saw a familiar hand clamp itself over the exit end of the tube. Twisting the warrior around to face him, Indy pressed his own lips to the weapon and blew forcefully into it. Mutt could hear the dart slam into the back of the warrior's throat. Staggering backwards, he dropped the blowgun, gasped, then fell like a tree, his eyes rolling back into his head.

Seeing this, the first warrior, now armed with the bloodied switchblade, lunged at Mutt. But Indy was just warming up. In a flash, he had jerked the bullwhip from his belt and sent it flying for the warrior's arm. A flick of his wrist, and the knife was wrenched away. But the warrior was determined to go down fighting. Wiggling free of the whip, he was about to throw himself at Indy when he saw the revolver — Indy's revolver — the hammer already cocked. Then, pivoting through a nimble turn, he vanished into the shadows.

Mutt gazed up at Indy with wide eyes. Illuminated by lightning, wind tugging at his fedora and jacket, gun in one hand, bullwhip in the other, he might as well have stepped from a dime-store novel set in another century.

"Some teacher," Mutt said in awe.

"Well, I am," Indy said. "Part of the time."

Easing the revolver's hammer forward, he holstered the weapon. Mutt climbed from the tomb and retrieved the knife, a smear of blood darkening the blade.

"You know, I never actually used it before," he said absently.

"There's a first time for everything," Indy said. "You did all right." Relieving one of the corpses of its hat and poncho, he put them on the dead warrior and leaned him against a wall.

"That oughta keep him warm for a couple of hundred years." Looking around, Indy added, "They sure didn't like us poking around."

Mutt glanced around warily. "Man, who were those guys?"

"Custodians. Descendants of the Nazca warriors," Indy said. "Ox wasn't kidding when he wrote that Orellana's cradle was guarded by 'the living dead.'"

Following his nose now, Indy led them to the edge of the promontory the cemetery occupied, where a stone wall hollowed by niches prevented them going any farther. Cobwebs veiled the skulls and piles of bones in the niches, but there was no sign of a tomb.

"Dead end?" Mutt asked.

"I don't think so." Indy raised his chin in a nod. "Stone-work from two different eras. This part of the cemetery was constructed over a ruin."

On the ground four sets of footprints were impressed in the sand: two leading directly to the wall, and two away from it. Just above where the prints stopped was a niche containing a bare skull. The few cobwebs that remained over the nasal passages and jaws were moving, almost as if the skull were breathing.

Or were being stirred by air circulating behind the skull.

His eyes bright with sudden understanding, Indy poked his thumb and middle finger into the skull's eye sockets and pulled it free of the niche. The rear wall was perforated, and a piece of rope tied in a loop emerged from the hole. Reaching into the niche, Indy gave the loop a tug, and the stone wall parted, revealing a narrow passageway.

Not wasting a minute, Mutt began to crawl into the dark space, only to retreat before he was fully inside, his arms covered with scorpions. Cocking its tail, the largest of the bunch sent the barbed tip of its stinger straight into Mutt's arm.

CHAPTER FOURTEEN

I've been stung!" Mutt said. "Jeez, I'm gonna die out here!"

Indy stepped forward to help him brush the creatures off his arms. "Relax. They're only scorpions."

"Only? *Only?!* Look at my arm! It's already swelling!"

Indy took a look. "How big was the one that got you?"

"Huge." Mutt spread his hands in exaggeration.

"Good."

"What do mean, '*good*'? If you want to get rid of me, just say so!"

Indy frowned. "Look, kid, with scorpions, the bigger the better." Indy started into the passageway, but stopped to look back at Mutt. "But if you get stung by a small one, don't keep it to yourself."

Mutt rubbed his arm and shook his head in disbelief at Indy's indifference. Flicking open the switchblade, he followed Indy inside and was hurrying to catch up when the floor of the passageway gave way beneath him. His hands clawing for holds on the crumbling edges of the three-foot-deep pit he had created, he cried out for help. He was sinking deeper into the hole when Indy hauled him back onto firmer ground.

"We're on a promontory," Indy said in reprimand. "The underside of this area of the cemetery has been eroded. Unless you're careful, you're going to find yourself plastered all over the Nazca Lines."

"Now there's a pretty picture," Mutt said once he had caught his breath. "And, yeah, thanks for the advice," he added as Indy was moving away.

Mutt followed him down a long flight of stone steps into a small chamber. With Indy's body shielding the lantern light, the darkness was so thick Mutt couldn't see his hand in front of him. Squinting, he could just make out Indy's profile. He had his hand extended to touch Indy on the shoulder when Indy turned and the lantern illuminated three ancient skeletons bound in fetal positions, their hollow eye sockets squirming with insects.

Mutt loosed a startled scream, but not out of fear. "Their skulls, man!"

Indy was suddenly beside him. "Keep it down, will ya?"

Mutt pointed to the skeletons. "Look at their skulls!"

Indy raised the lantern. The foreheads of the skulls

were sloped and the craniums were elongated in the rear, almost egg-shaped.

"Like the one Ox drew," Mutt said.

Indy nodded in a satisfied way. "Which means we're on the right track."

Deeper in, they came to a tunnel that forced them down on hands and knees. But the chamber at the end of the tunnel had headroom enough for them to stand. Indy was extending the lantern in front of him when Mutt crawled into the room and approached from behind. Without warning, Indy's other arm shot out, stopping Mutt in his tracks.

"Stay put and don't touch a thing. Understand?"

Mutt stood still. "Whatever you say."

Indy passed the lantern across the ground, where once more four sets of footprints were impressed in the sand, two leading into the chamber, and two leading out.

"Same size. Could have been the same person, twice," Mutt remarked.

"Not bad, kid," Indy said.

The prints ended at a low earthen wall, against which rested several bundles wrapped in silvery cocoons and an antique treasure chest. Careful to avoid marring the footprints, Indy went to the wall. Bending down, he fingered open the foil wrapping of the nearest bundle, then pulled it back to reveal another layer — and two more beneath that one. Ultimately, however, the body of an armor-clad, bearded conquistador was revealed, half-a-millennia old but in a state of near-perfect preservation.

Indy turned and did a head count of the cocoons. "Seven!" He gripped Mutt's uninjured forearm in surprise. "It's them! Orellana and his men. They made it out of the Amazon after all, only to end up buried."

Mutt stared at the conquistador in awe. "He looks like he died yesterday."

Indy nodded. "Everything's intact — clothes, skeleton, skin ..." He fingered the silvery foil. "I've seen this stuff before. Ten years ago, at a crash site in New Mexico. And a few weeks ago in Nevada." Tearing a piece loose, he crushed it underfoot and watched it resume its original shape.

Mutt gazed in wonderment.

In one of the conquistador's gauntleted hands was a golden dagger with a jewel-encrusted hilt. Pulling the dagger free, Indy held it up to the lantern light, a gleam in his eye. He was about to stow it in his satchel when Mutt cleared his throat in a meaningful way.

"Uh, you did say something about us not being grave robbers."

Indy blinked, then looked at Mutt. "I wasn't planning on keeping it."

"'Course you weren't."

Indy turned back to the cocoon to replace the dagger and gave a start. In seconds, the conquistador's flesh and sinew had aged five hundred years. Skin the texture of parchment was now stretched across bone; the hair had lost its sheen; the fingernails had grown long and thick, like yellowed ivory.

As Mutt leaned in for a closer look, the switchblade flew from his hand and fastened itself to the magnetic wrapping.

"Put that thing away," Indy said, scowling at him.

Leaving Mutt to pry the knife free, he went to the chest, opened the lid, and removed one of the coins that filled the interior. "Bronze," he said, flipping the coin over. "Athena. What d'you know. These aren't Spanish. They're Macedonian. Three hundred B.C. or earlier." He raised the lantern in puzzlement. "Orellana wouldn't have brought them here. So what are they doing in a temple in South America?"

Indy moved to the second of the seven cocoons and carefully parted the layers of foil, watching in amazement as the conquistador contained inside transformed into a mummy.

Mutt called him from the far side of the crypt. "Here's one that's already been opened!"

Indy joined him. Not only had the cocoon been opened, a mask of gold had been placed over the conquistador's face.

"The Gilded Man," Indy said. "Francisco de Orellana himself." He touched the mask, his brow furrowing. "Something's not right. Whoever buried him wouldn't have deliberately covered his face. The Nazca knew that the Spanish didn't wear burial masks. Unless . . ."

Indy wedged his fingers around the edges of the mask, then moved them around to the back of the conquistador's skull and pulled the entire corpse forward so that it was practically in Mutt's lap, face-to-face with him. Behind the body, his hands found a second skull, which he pulled into the scant light.

Fashioned from one piece of what was perhaps quartz, the skull's eyes were lensed — and enormous. The chin was pointed and the teeth were too small and too many in number. At the center of the cranium glowed a second, opalesque crystal. When Indy held the skull close to the lantern, the facets of the carving both refracted and absorbed the light, directing it to the eyes, from which rainbow light streamed, as if from a prism.

Indy marveled. "No tool marks, no evidence of a lapidary wheel, cut against the grain . . . This isn't possible, not even with today's technology. The stone would shatter." He turned the skull about in his hands in order to study its elongated rear. "Nothing at all like any skull I've ever seen."

"You think Orellana stole it from Akator?" Mutt said. "But maybe the Nazcans didn't know, so they just buried it with him?"

Indy glanced over his shoulder at the sets of footprints. "Could be, kid." He gestured to the silvery wrappings and the chest of coins. "And maybe they looted the rest of this stuff from Akator while they were at it." He fell silent for a moment. "Headed back to their ships anchored off the coast. Greed could've gotten the better of them along the way . . . Whatever happened, the locals found them, wrapped them up, and buried them here with all their loot."

"But why is the crystal skull here?" Mutt asked.

Indy shrugged. "Ox must have found it here and returned it for some reason before he headed for Akator."

"Return," Mutt started to say, then sucked in his breath and pointed to Orellana's body. Indy whirled in time to see the conquistador's gauntleted hand begin to rise from the body, almost as if Orellana was reaching out for the skull.

Indy frowned. The higher he raised the skull, the higher the hand climbed; and when he lowered it, the hand lowered as well.

"It's not the arm," he said at last. "It's the armor."

Mutt's brows beetled. "Since when is crystal magnetic?"

"Good question," Indy said. Looking the skull in the eyes, he added, "So just what are you?"

As Indy continued to stare at the skull, a faint light came to life in the huge crystal eyes, brightening and intensifying with each passing second, to the point where Indy couldn't have torn his gaze away even if he had wanted to. Behind him, Mutt was growing equally transfixed, on the verge of slipping into what seemed a hypnotic trance when the ground suddenly gave way beneath his feet once more.

The sound was enough to break the skull's spell on Indy, who turned to find that this time Mutt had fallen completely through the floor of the crypt. His left hand was clamped on the armored leg of Orellana's skeleton, but his legs were dangling over the dark Nazca Plain hundreds of feet below. Quickly, Indy threw himself on Orellana's skeleton, which was being held together only by the thick leather straps that joined the separate pieces of armor. Mutt screamed as the armor began to slip down Orellana's leg, and bones from the disintegrating skeleton began to slide through the hole and vanish into the blackness below him.

By now Indy was face-first on the ground, with both arms wrapped around the upper carapace of the conquistador's body armor. The leather thongs were stretching to their limit, and the skull, which he had dropped, was suddenly rolling straight for the hole Mutt had opened in the eroded promontory.

"The skull!" Indy said, groaning as he watched it drop straight through the hole.

"Got it!" Mutt yelled an instant later.

Seeing the skull in Mutt's free hand, Indy put all of his strength into heaving Mutt up and out of the hole and back onto solid ground, even as the last of Orellana's bones and most of the armor fell into the night.

Grabbing the skull from Mutt, Indy scrambled to his feet and pulled Mutt to his. Then the two of them began to race back the way they had come, large sections of the floor collapsing behind them to rain down on the Nazca Lines.

Dawn was breaking when they finally emerged from the parted wall of the burial chamber. First out, Indy was clapping dust from his pants and jacket when he happened to look up, and the color drained from his face.

"Hello, old pal," Mac said to him from a few feet away. Dressed in a poncho and a wide-brimmed Panama hat, Mac was flanked by armed Russian soldiers, including Antonin Dovchenko.

Emerging from the passageway at Indy's back, Mutt

gave Mac the once-over before saying, "Who's this clown?"

Indy lunged, but to no effect. Eager to pick up where they had left off, Dovchenko brought the butt of his gun down on Indy's head, then did the same to Mutt, before he could even react. Both men crumpled to the ground. Then, lifting a stone from the ground, Dovchenko brought it up over Indy's head, but Mac stopped him before he could lower the boom.

"No. She said she needs him alive."

On the ground, Indy briefly stirred back to consciousness. The crystal skull had tumbled from his satchel, and just now he was eye to eye with it. And something was moving in those flat, otherworldly eyes, a light of sorts, born of something other than flame or the first rays of dawn.

Indy had scant time to reflect on it. A hand was approaching, in its blunt fingers a syringe, the tip of which plunged into Indy's neck.

"Here we go again," Indy said in a world-weary voice, while the skull watched him descend into blackness.

Indy was right. It was Mexico all over again, only this time it was Mutt beside him rather than turncoat Mac, and trains and boats in place of planes and trucks.

The drug the Russians had injected into his neck made him feel like a scuba diver decompressing from a deep dive, but unable to break the surface of the water. Periodically he would come to, but woozily and feeling adrift. For a time, his ears registered the *clack-clack* sound of moving train wheels, then a plaintive hooting sound that might have come from the horn of an old riverboat.

In a rare moment of clarity, he tried to work out where the Russians were taking them, in which direction and by which route. Based on the assumption his ears hadn't deceived him about the train wheels or the ship's horn, the choices were limited.

From his earlier travels in Peru, he knew that trains south from Nazca led to the White City of Arequipa, then east to Lake Titicaca, from which it was possible to descend the eastern slopes of the Andes and reach the Madre de Dios River, in the Amazon basin. North, the train line led to the highland town of Huancayo, from which it was also possible to reach the jungle by way of Pucallpa and the Ucayali River, which flowed north to Iquitos, on the Amazon.

But all this was nothing more than speculation. What mattered was that he and Mutt were alive, which meant only one thing: the Russians needed them.

CHAPTER FIFTEEN

*I*ndy was in desperate need of a drink, something to dribble down his parched throat and slake his thirst. Wetting his lips with his tongue, he lifted his chin from his chest. His eyes blinked open and the world came slowly into focus, illuminated by a single lantern. He was inside a large canvas tent, tied to a folding camp chair. The air was warm and thick enough to cut with a knife.

Jungle air. Amazonian jungle air.

A hand pressed a glass of clear liquid to his dehydrated lips, and he swallowed a couple of sips, the astringency of the liquid causing him to cough and nearly choke. His eyes found the bottle from which it had come, the Cyrillic lettering of the label.

Then he spit.

"Ugh! Disgusting."

He heard Mac's telltale laugh and looked up fully. His

erstwhile friend was seated in a chair opposite him. "This makes it three times I've saved your life, Indy."

Indy found the strength to grin. "Untie me, Mac, and I'll show you how I say thanks."

"You had a Luger pointed at the base of your skull the first time we met," Mac went on. "And of course there were the amnesia darts I pulled from your neck in Jakarta."

"Amnesia darts?"

"How quickly you forget. But take my word for it, Indy, you owe me. Back at Nazca, our friend Colonel Dovchenko was keen to crush your skull with a rather large rock."

"That, I remember," Indy said. "But tell me something, Mac. After the war, when you turned, how many names did you give the Reds? How many good men died because of you? What do you owe *them*?"

Mac snorted. "I don't think you're seeing the big picture, mate."

Indy narrowed his eyes. "Eventually these ropes are coming off, and when they do, the first thing I'm going to do is break your nose, *comrade*."

Mac put his hands on his knees and laughed. "*Comrade?* Indy, do you actually believe I care about these Reds? Or uniforms of any sort, for that matter?"

Mac cut his eyes to the right, and Indy followed his gaze to a small table, atop which a reel-to-reel tape recorder was running in record mode. "I remember that, too, Mac," he said at last. "The only thing you care about is money."

"Not just money, Indy. A *gigantic pile* of money." He blew out his breath. "Forget what these Russians are paying me. It's nothing compared to what waits for us at Akator." He leaned forward in the chair. "An entire city of gold, Indy. Think about it. It's what the conquistadors were after, for God's sake. We'll be richer than Howard Hughes."

"Blood money," Indy said. "Every nickel of it."

Mac took a moment to glance over his shoulder. When he spoke again, his voice took on a conspiratorial tone.

"I need you to see the angle here, mate. Be smart and play your part. Just like in —"

Mac paused briefly. The mesh flaps of the tent had parted forcefully, stirring a breeze that threatened the lantern's small flame. Standing at Mac's back an instant later was Irina Spalko, wearing Russian military fatigues and her signature rapier.

Still facing Indy, Mac emphasized in a low voice, "*Like in Berlin*, get me?"

Abruptly, he stood up, turned, and exited the tent, leaving Spalko to size Indy up, her arms crossed in front of her.

"How fortunate we were in failing to kill you in Nevada, Dr. Jones," she began. "You survive to be of service once again."

Indy shrugged. "You know me, anything I can do to help."

Spalko was silent for a moment, then said, "'Now I am become death, destroyer of worlds.' Surely you recognize those words. They came from your own Dr. Oppenheimer, after he helped design the atomic bomb."

"He was quoting Hindu scripture," Indy said. "The *Bhagavad Gita*."

"First the atomic bomb, then the hydrogen bomb. What your Presidents Truman and Eisenhower did to the Russian people was nuclear intimidation. But we were not as backwards as some American scientists thought. We reached parity with you more quickly than anyone thought we could. And now, Dr. Jones, we are on the brink of surpassing you, using technology your countrymen haven't had the sense to recognize. A weapon America will fear as Russia once feared the bomb."

Indy stared at her. "If you're talking about that crystal skull —"

"The skull is a mind weapon. It will open a new frontier of psychic warfare. It was Stalin's dream."

Indy smirked. "Now I see why Oxley put it back where he found it. He knew you people were after it."

Spalko lowered herself into the chair Mac had vacated and helped herself to a glass of vodka. "You look at me as if I'm insane, Dr. Jones, but I'm anything but. That skull is not a simple deity carving. As I am sure you have already realized, it was not fabricated by human hands."

"Then whose hands made it?"

Spalko gestured to a coffinlike object near the door of the tent. Indy recognized it as the container the Russians had stolen from Hangar 51.

"The body we liberated from your warehouse wasn't the first we had seen. We had already dissected two others from crash sites in the Soviet Union."

"Saucer men from Mars?" Indy said, restraining an impulse to smile.

"The legends about Akator are true, Dr. Jones. Humans could not have conceived it, much less built it." Spalko studied him. "It was a city of supreme beings, with technologies and paranormal abilities."

"You've got to be kidding me."

"You were described to me as a professor of archaeology, an expert on the occult, an acquirer of rare antiquities, and yet, why do you choose not to believe your eyes? There's no other explanation."

"There's always another explanation."

"The skull was stolen from Akator in the fifteenth century. Whoever returns it —"

Indy interrupted her. "— to the city's temple gets control over its power. I've heard that bedtime story, too. But what if Akator doesn't exist?"

Spalko smiled. "You should ask your friend that question. We're certain Professor Oxley has been there."

Indy strained at his bindings. "Ox is here?"

Spalko's smile didn't falter. "In a fashion, yes."

Sandwiched between two Russian soldiers when he emerged from the tent, Indy was astonished to see the resources the Kremlin or the KGB or maybe the Red Army had placed at Spalko's disposal. Even in the negligible light of lanterns and campfires, Indy counted more than two dozen additional soldiers and, parked along the perimeter of the jungle camp the Russians had cleared, an array of military vehicles, including jeeps, trucks, amphibious craft similar to the American-made DUKW, and a monstrosity designed to level trees and mulch vegetation.

But there was no sign of Oxley, at least not until Spalko, Dovchenko, and Mac directed Indy's attention to a figure gyrating around one of the campfires like a Native American engaged in a ritual peyote dance, much to the amusement of tipsy soldiers who were urging him on with enthusiastic clapping and laughter.

Indy's jaw and shoulders dropped. It was Oxley, all right, bearded and wearing campesino pants, a long, faded shirt, and a tall-crowned hat whose band was adorned with tropical bird feathers. His graying hair was long and stringy, and his red-rimmed eyes shone madly in the firelight.

If Indy's hands hadn't been tied, he might have hurried to embrace his old friend. But all he could do was call out to him.

"Ox, it's me — Indy! You remember me, dontcha, pal?" Indy stepped through the circle of boisterous soldiers to place himself in Oxley's path. "You're faking it, right? Tell me you're pulling a fast one on these chumps."

Oxley ceased dancing, but his eyes refused to meet Indy's. "*'Through eyes that last I saw in tears...'*" he intoned. "*'Through eyes that last I saw in tears...'*"

Up close, Indy noticed that Oxley's right hand was twitching uncontrollably. "Listen to me," he said in a firmer voice. "You're Harold Oxley. You were born in Leeds and you were never half this interesting. You and I attended the University of Chicago together. One of our professors was named Ravenwood. Remember? I'm Indy. Henry Jones . . . uh, Junior. No way you could forget me, right?"

But apparently Oxley had. Spinning away, he resumed his dance around the fire, muttering unintelligibly to himself all the while.

Indy whirled on Spalko and Mac. "What did you do to him?"

"We didn't do a thing," Mac said, providing the answer Indy already knew. "It was that bloody skull that did this to him."

Spalko glanced from Oxley to Indy. "He's a psychic miracle, Dr. Jones. A divining rod that will lead us to Akator." She glanced at Oxley again before continuing. "However, we need someone to interpret him for us." She trained her eyes on Indy. "You will help him remember the way to Akator."

Spalko nodded to Dovchenko, who delighted in clamping his hands on Indy's arms.

"Oxley's mind is quite weak," Spalko added. "Let's hope that yours is stronger."

Quicker than he could say uh-oh, Indy was dragged into a larger tent and strapped into a chair. Spalko, Mac, and Dovchenko gazed at him in expectation while two soldiers attached electrodes to his temples and forehead. Wires ran from the electrodes to an electro-encephalogram running on generator power.

A table was placed in front of Indy, and on it, Spalko set the crystal skull, which was wrapped in the same silver foil Indy had seen in Hangar 51 and Chauchilla Cemetery.

Bits of metal shavings leaped to cling to the foil as Spalko peeled it away from the skull, and the hands on the soldiers' wristwatches spun clockwise and counterclockwise.

"Missing for five hundred years," she mused, "and fated to come into our hands." Spalko nodded to a soldier, who switched on the EEG monitor. "The New Mexico specimen gave us hope," she went on. "Unlike the other bodies we found, its skeleton was *pure* crystal."

Fully revealed now, the flat-eyed skull caught the light of the lanterns and embellished it.

Spalko gazed at the skull. "A distant cousin of the original visitors, perhaps. Maybe they, too, were dispatched to find Akator. Perhaps we're all searching for the same thing."

Behind her, two soldiers wheeled a 30-caliber machine gun into the tent.

Indy gaped at it. "Hey, even I'm not *that* tough," he said.

Spalko smiled at him. No sooner did the soldiers lift the gun from its tripod than she replaced the gun with the skull, rotating it to face Indy. "The unique quality of the crystalline structure stimulates an undeveloped part of the human brain, opening a psychic channel," Spalko said succinctly. "Professor Oxley stared too long into its eyes and went mad. I want you to go just mad enough to communicate with him."

Placing a hand on Indy's face, she began to stroke his cheek with her fingertips, enticing him to turn his face to the skull.

"I got a better idea," Indy said. "You stare at it."

Sadness darkened Spalko's smile. "I've tried and failed. Many have. The skull's sensory motor rhythms appear to be suited to a select few."

At Nazca Indy had glimpsed something in the skull's eyes; now, however, the outsize eyes appeared to be glowing with eager intensity.

When the slender needles on the EEG jumped, Spalko perked up.

"Surely you're not afraid, Dr. Jones," she said in elaborate concern. "After all, you've spent your entire life searching for answers to our deepest mysteries. Just think of the truths this ancient artifact will be able to impart. Think of the truths that reside in these crystal eyes."

Indy gritted his teeth. "Like I told you before, I'm not interested in truth, only fact."

He had more in mind to say, but his thoughts were silenced by a sudden pulsing from the skull, a sudden brightness in its eyes. Despite his best efforts, Indy was unable to look away. He found himself being drawn into the skull, Spalko's soft caresses abetting his surrender.

The EEG needles began a spastic dance, drawing mad zigzags on the monitor's paper scroll.

"There could be hundreds of such skulls at Akator," Spalko was saying. "Perhaps thousands. And whoever finds them will control the greatest natural force the world has ever witnessed: power over the mind of every human being."

Indy's eyes were fixed on the skull. "Be careful. You might get exactly what you ask for," Indy muttered.

"I usually do."

Yet again the fire in the disk-shaped eyes intensified, though that hardly mattered since Indy was already hopelessly transfixed.

"Imagine being able to peer across the world and know the secrets of your enemies," Spalko said, as if from a great distance. "Then to be able to place your thoughts in the minds of your enemy's leaders. To be able to compel your children's educators — educators like yourself, Dr. Jones — to teach the true version of history. To be able to compel your soldiers to defend *our* people."

Indy's heartbeat throbbed in his temples. He wanted desperately to respond to Spalko, but his voice failed him, and the EEG needles registered his inner turmoil.

"We will be everywhere at once, Dr. Jones, as powerful as a whisper, a hypnotic command, thinking your thoughts for you while you sleep. Planting the seeds of a new world order. We will change you — all of you. From the inside.

We will turn you into us. One world with one mind. A collective unconscious. And the best part: you won't even be aware of it."

Indy began to tremble, his eyes bulging slightly in his flushed face. Capillaries stood out in the whites of his eyes.

"This skull is a destroyer of worlds, Dr. Jones — *your* world. And it will be the beginning of ours. There will be no us and them," Spalko said in conclusion. "Only us."

The dilated capillaries in the whites of Indy's eyes burst as tears of blood, and the EEG needles began to find a steady rhythm. Spalko studied the printout in awe.

"His brain waves are off the chart. He has attained a full hypnagogic state."

Indy's eyes were glued to the skull. In the voice of a zombie, he said, "*Return . . .*"

At the campfire, Harold Oxley suddenly stopped dancing and turned to face east. "*Return*," he intoned.

In the tent, two trickles of blood leaked from the corners of Indy's eyes and began to course down his cheeks.

And out in the night, Oxley touched his cheeks, as if to wipe away tears.

"Henry," he said softly.

Seeing the streaks of blood on Indy's face, Mac placed his hands on Spalko's shoulders, shaking her out of her trance. "Snap out of it, woman, that's enough! We never find Akator if he dies!"

Spalko didn't respond immediately. Then, pointing to the skull, she said, "Cover it! Cover it!"

Quickly, one of the soldiers stepped in to drape a square of dark cloth over the skull. The link broken, Indy blinked but didn't alter his gaze.

"You think he's all right?" Mac asked in genuine concern.

Spalko and Dovchenko leaned toward Indy. "Dr. Jones?" she asked.

Indy's expression remained blank.

"He's under the spell of the skull," Spalko said in full confidence. She signaled Dovchenko to undo the straps that bound Indy to the chair. "Hurry! We must bring Jones and Oxley together!"

Dovchenko started with the strap that restrained Indy's right arm. No sooner was it undone than Indy's clenched fist flew from his side, directly into Mac's nose, which issued a loud *crack!*

Mac fell back violently, his hands pressed to his face. "You broke my nose!" he said in a muffled voice.

"You can't say I didn't warn you," Indy snarled.

Grabbing hold of Indy's free arm, Dovchenko slammed him back down into the chair.

"Enough of this!" Spalko said in exasperation. Coming eye to eye with Indy, she added, "You will now speak with Dr. Oxley. You will lead us to Akator."

"I'd sooner lead you off a cliff."

Expecting no less, Spalko barked an order to the soldiers, who immediately moved in on Indy.

CHAPTER SIXTEEN

*I*ndy was more affected by his intimate contact with the crystal skull than he let on. Many of his cheeky replies to Spalko's musings about the paranormal had been nothing more than bluster. In fact, for most of his life he had wrestled with the very questions she had put to him. He had seen many amazing things in his lifetime, but he had always considered himself to be as much a scientist as an adventurer, and he had constructed complex rationalizations to explain each mystery. But his stance had softened somewhat over the course of the past fifteen years. Where he had once believed that X never marked the spot, and that items like the Ark of the Covenant and the Grail cup had never existed, he had become more openminded. Or at least he liked to think so.

As Spalko and Mac were escorting him from the tent, Indy asked himself: What was the harm in believing, as Spalko did, that the crystal skull could bestow power of a paranormal sort? What was he fighting? Was he afraid of giving in?

From a separate tent two soldiers dragged Mutt out into the night.

"You okay, kid?" Indy called out.

Mutt looked at him in wide-eyed disbelief. "They left my bike at that Nazca cemetery!"

Indy nodded. "Yeah, I know. But are you okay?"

Mutt grew even more incredulous. "Did you hear what I said? They left my bike!"

A soldier carrying a two-by-four-foot case of polished cherrywood approached Spalko, who handed him her rapier. Unsnapping the case's lid, the soldier wedged the sword into a molded setting in the velvet interior. In turn, Spalko lifted an evil-looking foil from its setting, flicked the blade through the air several times, and leveled it at Mutt.

Mutt raised his hands in surrender. "Wait, don't," he started to say, then paused to pull his comb from the back pocket of his blue jeans and run it through his hair, shaping the rear into a perfect ducktail. Finished, he showed Spalko a look of utter fearlessness. "Okay, go ahead." Glancing at Indy, he added, "Don't give these Reds a thing."

Indy shook his head in admiration. "You're got pluck, kid." Then he turned to Spalko. "You heard him. I'm not supposed to give you a thing."

"American heroes," Spalko said in disgust, then smiled. "Clearly I've chosen the wrong pressure point, Dr. Jones. Perhaps, however, I can discover a more sensitive one." She swung to her soldiers. "*Privedite zhenshchinu!*"

The soldiers saluted and ducked into a nearby tent. A commotion followed, as the soldiers attempted to hustle the tent's uncooperative occupant into the open.

Then a woman's voice shouted, "Take your hands off me, you rotten Ruskie rats!"

Indy's body went rigid and his jaw dropped. He knew that voice almost as well as he knew his own, and a vivid image of the woman it belonged to leaped into his mind even before the Russians succeeded in hauling her, cursing and kicking, from the tent. He hadn't seen her in two decades, but judging by appearances, the intervening years had been kinder to her than they had been to him. Even here, in the sweltering Amazon, her clothes in disarray and her black hair disheveled, Marion Ravenwood was the same lithe, freckle-faced spitfire he had fallen in love with — twice — and abandoned — twice. And the memory of the way they had ended made his heart ache and his head hurt worse than it did from staring into the eyes of the crystal skull.

"Marion!" Indy exclaimed.

Seeing Indy, Marion stopped her useless struggling to

eye him head to toe. "Well, it's about time you showed up, Jones."

"Mom!" Mutt said in sudden relief.

Marion turned to him in annoyed surprise. "Sweetheart! What in the world are you doing here?"

Indy glanced at Mutt, then Marion, then Mutt again. "*Mom?*"

"Ah, don't worry about me," Mutt told Marion. "Are you all right?"

Indy stammered. "*Marion* is your . . ."

"Young man, I specifically told you . . ."

". . . your mother?"

". . . not to come down here."

"Marion Ravenwood is your mother?!"

"I should've known Jones would drag you into this."

"*Marion Ravenwood is your mother?!*"

Marion turned to Indy, tugging at the tan vest that matched her pants. "For cryin' out loud, Jones, is it so hard to figure out?"

Indy stared at her. "I just . . . I never . . . I didn't think you'd . . ."

"Didn't think I'd what — have a life after you left me? Well, guess again, buster."

Indy shook his head. "That's not what I —"

"I've had a pretty good life, Jones."

Indy swallowed. "That's great. I just —"

"A darn good life, in fact."

Something in Marion's tone snapped Indy out of his amazement. "Oh, yeah? Well, so have I."

"Oh, I don't doubt that," Marion said, grinning. "But tell me, Jones, you still leaving a trail of human wreckage in your wake, or have you retired from womanizing?"

Indy narrowed his eyes. "Why, you looking for a date?"

"Um, speaking of dates," Mac suddenly interrupted. "I'd be more than happy to show you around the camp."

Marion turned slowly, giving Mac her most withering look, then said to one of the soldiers, "How about letting go of me so I can punch this son-of-a —"

"What are you mad at me for?" Indy asked.

"How much time do you have?" Marion gulped down the rest of it as the soldier responded by pressing the barrel of his sidearm to her temple.

Approaching Marion, Spalko waved the soldier away and brought the tip of the foil close to Marion's eye. "Perhaps you will help us now, Dr. Jones," she said, looking at Indy. "A simple 'yes' will suffice."

Indy laughed ruefully. "You just had to go and get yourself kidnapped, Marion. Again."

She frowned at him. "Doesn't look like you did any better, Jonesy."

* * *

Having danced himself into a state of exhaustion, Oxley was resting by the campfire, staring blankly at the surrounding jungle when Mac ambled over to set up the reel-to-reel tape recorder and position the microphone.

"Interested in a little action on the interview?" Mac asked one of the soldiers. When the soldier nodded, Mac pulled from his pocket a wad of American dollars, Peruvian *soles*, and British pounds. "I'm giving three-to-one odds that the Yank figures Oxley out."

"I take the bet," the soldier said.

Spalko led Indy to the campfire and motioned for him to sit down opposite Oxley. Indy took a deep breath, but before he could say a word, Oxley turned to him, recognition in his eyes.

"Henry Jones, Junior!"

Encouraged suddenly, Indy said, "That's right, Ox. It's me, Henry. Now, listen closely —"

"Henry Jones, *Junior*!" Oxley clamped his hands on Indy's upper arms, as if struggling to communicate something he was incapable of verbalizing. "*'To lay their just hands on that Golden Key,'*" he said, as if reciting verse, "*'that opes the Palace of Eternity.'*"

Indy couldn't make rhyme or reason of it. "The Palace of —"

"It's a quote from Milton," Spalko interrupted. "He has said it before. What does he mean?"

Indy forced a breath. "I teach archaeology, not literature."

Spalko's upper lip curled. "I will be sure to tell Mrs. Williams how hard you tried to save her face."

Indy gazed at her. "Colder than Siberia."

Spalko lifted her chin to Oxley. "Try again."

Indy nodded and turned slightly to face Oxley head-on. "Harold, I know that you've been to Akator. Now I need you to tell me how to get there."

Oxley looked haunted. His right hand began to twitch, as it had done during his dance. "*Through eyes that last I saw in tears . . . Here in death's dream kingdom . . .*'"

"Ox!" Indy snapped. "You remember Abner Ravenwood, don't you? He was our professor. If you don't tell me how to reach Akator, these people are going to kill Abner's daughter, Marion. Abner's little girl, Ox. You've got to tell me."

Oxley's urgency was palpable, his hand twitching without letting up. But the right words failed him once more. "*Eyes! That last I saw in —*'"

"How do we reach Akator, Ox? You've got to give me specific . . ." Indy paused for a long moment to watch

Oxley's hand, the fingers of which were pinched together, as if holding a utensil. "Somebody get me a pen and some paper!" he said finally.

Seconds later, a notebook and pen appeared. Positioning the pen in Oxley's palsied hand, Indy flipped the notebook open to a blank page and held it under the pen.

"Henry Jones, Junior!" Oxley said, holding Indy's gaze. But his pen hand was moving as well, not writing but drawing. "*Three times* it drops, Henry," he added, as if in confidence. "Three times it drops . . ."

Indy twisted his head to one side to regard the series of wavy lines Oxley's hand had drawn. Quickly, he flipped the page so that Oxley could continue writing on a fresh sheet. He watched as a pair of closed eyes took shape.

"Auto writing," Spalko said. "I should have grasped as much. This is how he managed to pen the letter you deciphered. He dwells in the collective unconscious. He thinks in *symbols.*"

Oxley's hand wasn't slowing down. Indy turned over a third page, just in time to catch Oxley's drawing of the sun arcing across the sky; then a snake with its tongue extended; then what appeared to be a horizon line.

"Pictographs?" Spalko asked in excitement.

Indy shook his head. "I don't think so. More like ideograms, like the ones he included in the letter."

He pulled the letter from his jacket pocket and, unfolding it, began to compare Oxley's notebook jottings to those on the page.

Mutt quickly stepped in and attempted to comfort Oxley. "Look at me, Ox. *Please*." His eyes began to brim with tears. "Please, Ox." Still, Oxley refused to meet his gaze.

Indy looked from Mutt to Spalko, and then to his notes. "Wavy lines usually represented water," he explained. "A closed eye meant sleep. The sun moving through the sky . . . That could be interpreted as 'time' or 'duration.' Epigraphers sometimes read it as 'until.'"

Indy jabbed at the third sheet with his forefinger. "The snake and the horizon line are close together, which suggests a relationship or a single idea." He mulled it over for a moment. "The horizon line represents the edge of the world, but it isn't meant to be taken literally. Its common meaning is 'big' or 'great.'"

"C'mon, Ox, look at me, man!" Oxley still didn't turn to Mutt. Mutt's eyes filled with tears. "Please?"

Indy ignored Mutt and, running his hand down his face in concentration, continued with the translation. "The water sleeps . . . until the great snake . . ." His tone made it a question. Then he sat up straight. "Wait! Ox is just answering my question! These are directions!" He whirled to Spalko. "Map!"

Mac, beaming, turned to the Russian with whom he had made the bet. "Time to pay the piper."

The map, along with a flimsy folding table, was longer in arriving than the pen and notebook had been, but in no time Indy had the map unrolled and was running his finger across it. Behind him the sun was up, and golden rays of light streamed through the trees at the edge of the clearing. Spalko, Mac, Marion, Mutt, and Dovchenko were watching Indy's every move.

"The Great Snake," Indy said quietly, "the Amazon. But 'sleeps'...." He looked at Spalko. "Where are we?"

Spalko hesitated, then said, "Iquitos."

Indy's lip curled in a half smile. "I thought so."

He brought his face closer to the map to read the small print; then, with his head canted to one side, he began to circle the map, reading aloud the names of some of the Amazon's tributaries.

"Bingo!" he announced.

Spalko and Mac leaned in to peer at what Indy's finger was indicating.

"The Great Snake has to be the Amazon, but 'sleeps,' what river sleeps?"

Spalko jabbed her finger down on the map. "The Sono River," she said. "The word is Portuguese for 'sleep.'"

"Yes! Exactly!" Indy's finger traced a sinuous line across the map. "Ox is telling us to follow this stretch of the Sono, southwest to where it joins the Amazon." He stood up, as if emerging from a dream. "That area is terra incognita, barely explored, let alone mapped. If Akator exists, it stands to reason it would be there."

Making the most of everyone's distraction, and with deliberate casualness, Mutt had moved to one end of the folding table and now had his hands gripped on the edge.

"As for the rest of it," Indy was telling Spalko, "all that Milton Ox was muttering, well, I'm as in the dark as you are. 'A dream kingdom, eyes in tears, three times it drops . . .'" He gestured to the map. "Maybe the words relate to certain geographical features."

Spalko and Dovchenko leaned closer to the map.

Mutt, watching them closely, waited for the moment when their faces were directly over the far end of the table.

Then, putting everything he had into it, he upended the table, sending it slamming into the two Russians, and yelling at the same time for Indy, Marion, and Oxley to run.

CHAPTER SEVENTEEN

*M*arion remembered suddenly that when you were anywhere in the vicinity of Indiana Jones, you had to be quick on your feet. But twenty years of sedentary living had slowed her reflexes, so it was Mutt who jolted her into action, taking her hand, yanking her to her feet, and leading her past the Russians' military vehicles and into the jungle.

Indy had done the same with Oxley, and the two of them were slightly behind, Indy warning Mutt not to go any deeper into the jungle, but to stick close to the banks of the muddy-green and slow-moving river. Indy had once filled her ears with wild tales about the Amazon — about red-haired elves that led travelers down dangerous paths, freshwater dolphins that could assume human form, and prehistoric sloths that ate people for breakfast — and she wasn't planning to spend any more time here than was absolutely necessary, but at the moment the jungle seemed preferable to whatever cruel fate awaited them in the Russians' camp.

Marion knew from the start that going to South America was a risk, but with all Oxley had done for her over the years she had no choice in the matter. Some part of her had even relished the idea of going on an adventure of the sort that had been commonplace when she traveled the world with her father and, for a time, Jones. But she hadn't counted on being kidnapped — much less by Russians. They had found Oxley in a sanitarium in Nazca and grabbed him there; and they had taken her in Lima, fresh off the flight from Mexico City. It was immediately clear to her that Irina Spalko and Antonin Dovchenko were not to be trifled with. They were prepared to do whatever needed to be done. But when even threatening her life hadn't been enough to persuade Oxley to reveal what he knew about some crystal skull and a lost city, the Russians had allowed her to escape, for just long enough to mail a crazy letter Ox had written, and to call Mutt, instructing him to bring the letter to Jones.

She knew Jones would come, even without her having to spill the beans about Mutt being her son — and the rest of it. And sure enough Jones had showed up, looking as if nothing had changed in twenty years, including his clothes, the fedora, and that bullwhip of his.

And now here they were fleeing for their lives, just like in the old days, except the red-hot rounds sizzling through of the trees around them were coming from Soviet guns instead of Nazi ones.

Marion wasn't sure just how far they had run when Indy called out for Mutt to stop. Long enough, though, for the thorned foliage to have shredded their clothing and raised angry welts on their faces. The light was waning and the crescent moon was up, but she had no idea what time it was or in which direction they were heading.

Still keeping the river on their right, Mutt had led them through a narrow ravine into a tiny clearing.

"Kid, hold up," Indy said quietly as he came even with Marion.

Oxley, looking no less distracted than when she had first laid eyes on him weeks earlier, was a few steps behind.

"Harold," Indy snapped. "Try to keep up, will ya?"

For a long moment they stood perfectly still. From upriver came the sound of boot steps, and through the trees they could see a group of Russian soldiers with flashlights hurry past them on a stretch of white-sand beach.

"Not that I don't appreciate what you did back there," Indy continued long after the soldiers had passed, "but maybe you didn't get a good look at the map. We're in unknown territory."

"They have the skull," Mutt said, "they know the way to Akator. They don't need us anymore. They were gonna kill us."

"Maybe they know the way and maybe they don't. The point is, there isn't even an indigenous village within fifty miles east, west, or south of us. Our best bet is to lay low and try to pick our way back to Iquitos. There's a Peruvian police post there."

Mutt crossed his arms over his chest. "Well, somebody had to do something. And at least I came up with a plan. All you were doing was giving them exactly what they wanted!"

Glaring at him, Indy muttered, "This is intolerable."

"Mutt," Marion said sharply.

Mutt showed her a sheepish look. "I know, Mom. I didn't want to see you hurt any more than he did."

Marion was about to thank him, when she felt the ground go spongy under her feet, and all at once she was looking *up* at Mutt. Either he'd just had a growth spurt or —

"Don't move!" Indy shouted to Mutt, whose face reflected sudden bewilderment. "Stay right where you are."

Gazing down, Marion was surprised to find herself

and Jones thigh deep in fine sand. "What the —" she started to say.

"Don't move," Indy repeated. "Movement makes space, and space makes you sink deeper."

"Sink?" Marion said, gulping. Reflexively, she began to tug on her right thigh. "I think I can get out if —"

"Stop it," Indy barked. "You're fighting a vacuum. You might as well try to lift a car. Just stay . . . calm."

Marion watched the sand creep up to her hips. "Okay, okay, I'm calm. I'm sinking, but I'm calm."

"Quicksand!" Mutt said in dread.

Indy shook his head. "Dry sand pit. Quicksand is a viscous mix of mud, clay, and water. But despite its fluidity, it's not as dangerous as most people —"

"For Pete's sake, Jones," Marion cut him off, "we're not in one of your lecture halls!"

He cut his eyes to her. "Fine. But stop thrashing around. There's nothing to worry about, unless —"

With a loud *ka-foom!* a geyser of sand erupted between them and shot ten feet into the air. Her eyes widening in terror, Marion sank to her armpits.

"Void collapse," Indy said flatly. "Gently raise your arms over your head."

Mutt was pacing back and forth in front of them. "I'll find something we can use to pull you out!" He spun through a circle, then rushed off into the forest, leaving a bemused Oxley to stare at Marion and Indy.

"Ox," Indy said in a controlled voice. "Are you gonna just stand there, or are you gonna help us?"

Oxley blinked, said, "Help?" and turned and walked off.

Marion gazed at Indy, her eyes brimming with tenderness. She'd known him for more than thirty years. With the moonlight coming through the trees, the moment might have been romantic, if they weren't in danger of being buried alive.

It was now or never.

"Mutt can be a bit impetuous," she said after a moment.

Indy glanced at her. "Not the worst quality in a kid —"

A sudden second void collapse fountained more sand into the air, and they sank to their chins.

"Keep your arms raised," Indy said. "The kid'll be back soon . . ."

"About Mutt, Indy," Marion said, the weight of the sand against her chest making it difficult to speak. "He's —"

"A good kid. I know. And you should probably get off his back about completing school."

"Indy —"

"I mean, not everyone's cut out for it."

"Mutt . . . His . . . his . . . his name is Henry."

"Henry?" Indy's expression soured. "How could you do that to him?"

Marion took a breath. "Because he's your son, Indy."

Indy gaped at her.

"Henry Jones the third."

Indy angled his head away from her for a moment, then snapped it around in fury. "Why the hell didn't you make him finish school?!"

Before Marion could respond to the charge, something long and heavy but unidentifiable in the dark came sailing through the air and slammed down on the sand between her and Indy. Returned to the edge of the pit, Mutt was holding tight to the other end of whatever he had launched.

"Grab hold of it!" Mutt shouted. "I'll pull you out!"

As gently as she could, Marion locked her hands on the thing. It was round and cold in a familiar way, and it was no jungle liana. Which was why she wasn't surprised when Indy screamed.

"Are you nuts?!"

"Just grab it, Indy," Marion said.

"It's a SNAKE! And it's hissing at me!"

"C'mon, man," Mutt said. "It's just a rat snake!"

"Rat snakes aren't this big!" Indy said. "It's either a python or an anaconda! Go find something else! A vine, a branch, anything!"

"Hey, this place ain't no Sears and Roebuck, man." Mutt looked at Marion. "What's with him? I was starting to think he wasn't afraid of anything."

"Childhood trauma," she explained. "It happened in a circus tent."

"Circus train car!" Indy said.

She forced an exhale. "Sorry I didn't keep better notes, professor."

Indy's eyes were big enough to see in the darkness. "Maybe I can touch bottom . . ."

"Indy, there is no bottom," Marion said. "Now will you just shut up and grab it!"

"No, wait, really, I think I can feel the bottom . . ."

"Jones!" Marion and Mutt yelled simultaneously.

Practicality won out. Closing his eyes, Indy tightened his hands on the snake. Mutt spread his legs to improve his stance and had just begun to heave on the snake when the largest geyser thus far created a huge void around Marion and Indy. Mutt pulled with all his might and the two of them literally flew from the pit, landing on top of Mutt in a tangle of limbs.

The snake lost no time in slithering back into the forest, nor did Mutt in extricating himself from the human knot the three of them had formed.

"Afraid of snakes," he muttered to Indy. "You are one crazy old geezer."

Grinning, Marion rolled over on her stomach to see two pairs of black boots shining in the moonlight a foot from her eyes. Lifting her gaze, she saw two Russian soldiers looming over her and, behind them, Oxley, standing between Spalko and Indy's one-time friend, Mac.

"Why do you insist on doing everything the hard way, Indy?" Mac said.

Marion watched Oxley puff himself up with pride. "I brought help."

Behind her, Indy said, "Good job, Ox. From the sand pit to the Soviets."

One of the soldiers laughed and tossed aside an empty vodka bottle.

From beneath it, unseen by any of them, emerged an enormous ant, its antennae twitching in seeming anger.

CHAPTER EIGHTEEN

*J*ones had been right about one thing. The rugged terrain of the Sono River — an area of jungle-crowned mesas like those in the Angel Falls region of Venezuela — was essentially off the map. What roads the Russians found were overgrown tracks pushed in by lumber companies that had extracted the area's centuries-old mahogany and cedar trees. But even dense jungle yielded to Soviet ingenuity, and the cutting and mulching vehicle Spalko had requisitioned for the expedition opened roads where there were none.

Leading the convoy of trucks, jeeps, and amphibious vehicles, the mulcher was a wedding of tank and bulldozer. In place of a gun turret, the treaded chimera had a shedlike driver's compartment aft and a V-shaped prow, reminiscent of a locomotive's snow remover, fronted by a pair of spring-loaded and chain-driven gear-toothed cutting blades capable of chewing up a meter-thick tree in a matter of seconds.

The convoy had been traveling for more than a day now, following the twisting river toward its source in the highlands, and Spalko was pleased with the progress they had made, thanks in large measure to Jones and what he had been able to get out of Oxley. She was also pleased to find that she had been correct about Jones from the beginning. He was as predictable as a Russian winter. All she had had to do was entice him and apply pressure. The man was simply incapable of resisting a good puzzle. Spalko had recognized that in Nevada, and she had seen it in action when Jones was deciphering the drawings Oxley's shaking hand had executed. He might tell himself he had done it to save Marion Williams from coming to harm, but that was only half the story.

It was clear, too, that the desperate escape hadn't been Jones' idea. The young man, Mutt, feared that he and his mother were about to be killed. But that wasn't the case. Spalko hated to admit even to herself that she needed Jones for a while longer, and she needed the teenager and Marion Williams to make certain that Jones continued to do as Spalko ordered. Once they reached Akator, well, then she would have to reevaluate. Perhaps she would turn Jones over to the loving care of Colonel Dovchenko.

She had until then to prepare for what awaited them at the lost Ugha city. And that involved attempting to communicate with the crystal skull. She was convinced that the skull had communicated with Jones, despite the show of bravado Jones had put on for everyone. Perhaps his contact with the skull had helped in some way with the deciphering of Oxley's drawings. Whatever the case, she knew she wasn't mistaken about the power inherent in the skull. Oxley had been driven mad by it, and Jones' brain waves had shown him to be in an extrasensory state.

Spalko rode in the back of a truck that was keeping a safe distance from the jungle mulcher. McHale was in the front seat, and Oxley was behind her, muttering to himself as he watched the play of sunlight through the trees. The skull, now encased in a knotted burlap sack, sat a meter from her face. Leaning forward, she undid the knot that cinched the burlap and allowed the sack to fall and gather around the skull's lower jaw. Then, sitting back, she trained her gaze on the skull's platterlike eyes.

But nothing happened.

The skull's eyes held no glow, and Spalko heard only the deafening sound of trees being felled and reduced to chips.

She took a moment to glance over her shoulder at Oxley, who was still muttering unintelligibly. Returning her attention to the skull, she whispered, "Why him and not me?"

Then, taking the skull between her hands, she leaned closer to it, as if in an attempt to force it to commune with her.

"That thing seems to have a mind of its own," Mac remarked from the front seat. When Spalko narrowed her eyes at him, he added, "Choosy about who it talks to."

Holding her anger in check, she drew the sack up over the cranium and cinched it with a length of cord. Without further word, she climbed into the front of the truck and slid into the passenger seat.

"C'mon, it's all a crock, isn't it?" McHale said a moment later. "People stare at that thing, work themselves up into a state — self-hypnosis or something. But ESP? Not bloody likely."

Spalko was scarcely in the mood for conversation, but she relented. "Why not? Telepathy is our sixth sense. We've simply forgotten how to make proper use of it."

Mac glanced at her. "You actually think we're psychic."

"You're a gambler. Have you never played a hunch that proved correct? Or picked up the phone to find the person you were about to call already on the line? Is this coincidence or the transmission of bio-information by means we have yet to fully understand?"

"It's called luck," Mac said. "I know all about it, since mine's usually bad."

Spalko smirked. "What about the bond between mother and child?" She turned slightly in Mac's direction. "The Technical Directorate performed an experiment. We sent a submarine under the surface with a mother rabbit's litter on board. She remained on shore while one by one the baby rabbits were put to death."

Mac winced. "Lady, you need a new hobby."

"Miles away," Spalko continued, "the mother rabbit's EEG readings showed reactions at the very instant of death. There is a mind link between all living creatures. If we could control that link, we would have power over all nature."

Mac pivoted in the seat to face her fully, fairly leering at her. "Okay. Double or nothing on the fee you're paying me. What am I thinking right now?"

She waved her hand in a dismissive way. "Much too easy."

Mac grinned. "Other than that, I mean. C'mon, amuse me. I'm thinking of a question. What's the answer?"

Spalko was deadly serious when she set her gaze on him, her sea-blue eyes boring into his, as if they were weapons, rapiers. Summoning her will, she compelled him to maintain eye contact long past the point he wanted to.

Abruptly, she clamped her hand behind his neck and pulled him close to her.

"The answer to your question is: should I feel the slightest need."

Mac blanched.

Releasing him, Spalko turned to face forward. "He wanted to know if I plan to cut his throat once we reach Akator," she said for the benefit of the soldier at the steering wheel.

CHAPTER NINETEEN

*F*rom the rear of a truck at the tail end of the convoy rose a scream so riddled with rage, disbelief, and consternation it could actually be heard above the raucously buzzing blades of the jungle cutter.

A second later, Mutt added words to the scream, "You've got to be kidding me!"

As were Indy and Marion, he was sitting in the back of the covered truck, tied with rope to a strut that supported the canvas top. Central to everyone, Dovchenko was seated atop one of the dozens of wooden munitions crates that crowded the bed.

"My father was a British RAF pilot," Mutt continued in the same agitated voice. "He was a *war hero*! Not some . . . *school*teacher!"

"I'm sorry, sweetheart," Marion said. "Colin was your stepfather. We started dating when you were three months old. He was a good man, but he wasn't your father."

"Wait a minute," Indy butted in. "Colin as in *Colin Williams*. You married *him*? I was the one who introduced you two!"

Dovchenko rolled his eyes in boredom. "Americans," he muttered.

Marion looked at Indy. "You gave up your vote on who I married when you decided to break it off a week before our wedding."

Indy bit back whatever he had in mind to say and started again. "It just wasn't going to work, Marion. We both knew that. Who would want to be married to some-body who's gone half the time?"

"I did. And you would have known if you'd bothered to ask!"

Dovchenko said, "Will all of you please shut up!"

Indy ignored the entreaty. "Asked you what, Marion? To spend most of your life alone?"

She shook her head at him in disappointment. "Maybe I would have liked the peace and quiet. You didn't know. Why didn't you just ask me?"

"Mom —" Mutt tried to interrupt.

"Because I knew it was going to lead to an argument, and we never had an argument that you didn't win!"

Marion almost smiled. "Hey, Jones, it's not my fault if you can't keep up."

Indy frowned. "I was trying to keep from hurting you."

"Mom —" Mutt tried again.

"Yeah? Well, guess what? You failed. Didn't you ever wonder why Ox stopped talking to you twenty years ago? He hated that you ran out on me."

"Would you two stop it!" Mutt shouted.

Indy glanced from Mutt to Marion. "He's right. He shouldn't have to hear Mom and Dad fight."

Mutt whirled on him. "You're *not* my dad, okay?!"

Indy grinned. "Sorry, kid, but you bet I am. And I've got some news for you: you're going to finish school."

Mutt looked terror stricken. "What happened to 'There's not a darn thing wrong with motorcycle repairs and don't let anybody tell you any different'?"

"I wasn't your father then." Indy faced Marion again. "You should have told me, Marion. I had a right to know."

"You pulled a vanishing act, remember?"

"I wrote," Indy said quietly.

"A *year* later. By then, Mutt was born and I was married."

Indy considered it. "So why'd you bother telling me now?"

"I *thought* we were *dying!*"

Fed up, Dovchenko slammed his gun down on the bed of the truck and began to pull rags from one of the crates. Everyone flinched, including the driver, though he was quick to recover.

"Don't worry, there's still time," Indy said.

Twirling one of the rags in his hands, Dovchenko fashioned a gag and was intent on tying it over Marion's mouth. Doing so, however, required that he squat down next to Marion, well within reach of Indy's legs.

It was the moment Indy had been waiting for and he kicked with both feet, catching the big Russian squarely in the face. Dovchenko's tumble took him within reach of Mutt's feet, which shot out, sending Dovchenko back to Indy, who rendered him unconscious with a final two-footed kick.

Trading nods with Mutt, Indy said, "You still have that switchblade of yours?"

Drawing his legs close to his chest, Mutt prized the knife from the top of his boot and shoved it to Indy, who immediately sprang the blade and went to work on cutting the rope that secured his hands.

Freed, Indy hurried to Marion's side.

"I wasn't the only one who moved on," she said while he was sawing at her bindings. "I'm sure there were plenty of women for you over the years."

"A few," he confessed. "But all of them had the same problem. They weren't you, honey."

Marion felt her heart melt. And she might have kissed him if he didn't abruptly move out of range, his attention drawn to one of the crates. Opening the lid, Indy grinned, then raised his eyes to the truck's canvas cover and began to scramble up toward it.

The driver of the truck never saw it coming.

He was looking straight ahead, eyes on the road, when Indy came feetfirst through the open window and sent him flying to the far side of the cab. Indy made a grab for the steering wheel, but not in time. The truck swerved directly into a sturdy tree, killing the truck's engine and catapulting Indy and the driver into the dashboard. Kicking open the passenger-side door, Indy shoved the unconscious soldier out of the truck and set himself at the wheel.

The crash had thrown Marion and Mutt forward as well, and by the time they clambered into the front seat Indy had the truck going again.

"Good one, Jones," Marion said. "Especially at your age."

Indy smiled in a lopsided way. "A peck on the cheek, a slug on the jaw. Just like the old days."

The truck leaped into motion, accelerating to catch up with the rest of the Russian vehicles, which were spread out in a long arc where the road paralleled a broad curve in the Sono River.

"We have to get Oxley," Indy said, "get our hands on that skull, and get to Akator before Spalko does."

"Just like that, huh?" Mutt said.

"Marion, take the wheel," Indy said suddenly, and was already scampering into the back of the truck before she had a chance to move.

Mutt watched him for a moment, then turned to Marion. "What's he going to do next?"

Double-clutching, she shifted the truck into a higher gear. "I don't think he plans that far ahead."

Just then the barrel of a Soviet-made bazooka emerged from the back of the truck, poking between Mutt and Marion. Mutt pressed himself into the seat as Indy climbed back into the front of the truck, hoisting the weapon onto his shoulder.

"Scoot back a little more, will you, son?"

"Don't call me that!" Mutt said, even as he did what Indy asked.

With the convoy still maneuvering through the broad turn, Indy had multiple targets of opportunity. Pointing the bazooka out the passenger-side window, Indy hooked his finger around the trigger and fixed the jungle mulcher in his sights.

"I can blow a tune on this they won't forget," he told Mutt. "Still, you might want to cover your ears."

CHAPTER TWENTY

*I*rina Spalko saw something streak past the windshield, and the next thing she knew a fiery explosion was flinging parts of the jungle mulcher into the river and trees. Losing one of its treads, the vehicle spun toward the riverbank, exploding a second time as fire from the first strike spread to the fuel tank. Engulfed in flames and oily smoke, it ground to a sudden halt, only to be rear-ended by a truck and explode a third time. The final detonation was powerful enough to flip the mulcher upside down. Ripped from the front end, the toothed jungle cutters hurtled toward the convoy like runaway propeller blades.

Hearing one of the disks whiz overhead, Spalko ducked. Everything happened so fast, it took her a moment to grasp that half the vehicles in the convoy had rammed into one another in a chain-reaction pileup. When she looked behind her, she saw the contrail of a rocket grenade hanging in the humid air, issuing from the last truck in line.

"Jones!" she said through gritted teeth.

At the same time, she realized that the professor may have doomed himself, for even as she watched, one of the whirling blades from the mulcher was closing on the cab of the truck.

Frightening countless birds into sudden flight, a shrieking sound filled the air as the gear-toothed blade decapitated the front portion of the truck. But Spalko had witnessed too many instances of Jones' uncanny luck to trust that he had been killed. Cursing in Russian, she ordered the soldier at the wheel to swing the vehicle around. When that didn't happen quickly enough, she climbed into the back, then over the rear hatch, and threw herself onto the hood of the jeep that was next in line. Scurrying past the driver, she grabbed an automatic weapon from the rear seat and began firing rounds at the now roofless truck.

Scrunched down behind the steering wheel, still recovering from the roof-shearing encounter with the saw blade, Marion looked to Indy for ideas.

Raising himself up on the bench seat, he pointed to an amphibious vehicle in front of them. "Pull up alongside the duck!"

Marion stomped on the gas pedal while Indy hooked his bullwhip to his belt and Mutt clamped his hands on the dashboard. Two Russians in the open-topped duck heard the roar of the truck's engine and turned, raising their weapons, but Indy was already in the air by then. Leaping from the truck onto the flat front deck of the olive-drab duck, he hurled himself over the low windshield to grapple with the two soldiers.

Indy made short work of the pair, sending them flying in opposite directions from the duck, and signaled for Marion and Mutt to abandon the truck and leap aboard. Mutt looked over his shoulder in time to see Dovchenko make a last-minute grab for the steering wheel to keep the truck from careening off the road.

In the duck, Indy also caught a glimpse of Dovchenko's desperate maneuver and slammed his foot on the gas pedal, speeding past the all-but-out-of-control truck to come alongside the jeep that Spalko had effectively commandeered. On her feet in the rear, she was continuing to lay down swaths of deadly fire, which reduced the duck's windshield to shards seconds after Marion dragged Indy and Mutt down onto the bench seat. Indy braked hard, falling back in order to place a second Russian jeep between Spalko's and the duck, but the sight of her own soldiers scrambling for cover didn't give her any pause.

Continuing to use the second jeep as protection, Indy accelerated again, whizzing past Spalko to come abreast of the convoy's lead truck, which carried Mac and Oxley, along with a couple of soldiers. Indy weaved the duck through the trees, waiting for intervening foliage to blind the truck's driver before yielding the wheel to Marion and launching himself toward the truck.

The driver felt the full impact of Indy's dive. Knocked from behind the wheel, he flew headfirst over Mac's lap directly into the passenger-side door. Mac swung to Indy, but only to have his nose reintroduced to Indy's fist.

"Ah, you broke my nose again!" he wailed, collapsing against the dashboard.

Indy had no sympathy for him. "It looked a bit out of joint, anyway," he said. With his left hand clamped to the steering wheel, he hauled Mac to him with his right, shielding himself from a soldier in the rear, who was leveling a rifle at Indy's head.

"Don't shoot!" Mac yelled.

And for some reason the Russian didn't, providing Indy with the time he needed to send the truck up and over a toppled tree, and throwing the armed soldier and his unconscious comrade into the air. The burlap bag containing the crystal skull also flew from the rear seat, but Oxley caught it, almost casually, and pulled it tightly to his chest. Behind him, however, and unknown to Indy, the soldier who had nearly shot him had managed to cling to the back of the truck and was slowly making his way back inside.

Still steering with his left hand, Indy cocked his right to hurl at Mac, when Mac said, "You idiot! I'm CIA!"

Indy's fist stopped in mid-flight.

"I practically shouted it to you in the tent," Mac continued nasally. "I said, *'Like in Berlin.'* And what were we in Berlin, mate? *Double agents*, yeah?"

Still dubious, Indy kept his fist raised.

Behind them, the Russian soldier had finally managed to haul himself into the rear. Seeing him, Spalko yelled for him to find the crystal skull. Before Indy or Mac could react, the soldier had snatched the burlap sack from Oxley's grip and sent it sailing for Spalko's jeep, an instant short of being knocked from the truck by Mac's fist.

Dropping back into the seat, Mac composed himself. "You think General Ross just *happened* to be in Nevada to bail you out? I sent him. He's my control. You were up to your blasted neck in KGB, and I kept you out of jail."

Indy relaxed his hand. "Why didn't you just tell me straight out?"

"What should I have done — painted it on my forehead?"

*　　*　　*

Spalko had the crystal skull but, against her earlier decision, she was determined to have Indy's head as well. Tossing aside the depleted rifle, she ordered the driver to pour on all speed and drew her rapier. Indy was weaving the truck evasively, but Spalko's vehicle was faster. She was a swing away from decapitating Indy when her keen senses alerted her to hidden danger, and she whirled. Something hissed through the air and, in the blink of an eye that something sliced through the front of her fatigues and opened a shallow gash across her abdomen.

A foil! she realized.

Her foil, and now in the right hand of Mutt Williams, who had discovered it in the cherrywood case in the rear of the duck. Standing in the front seat of the amphibious vehicle, Mutt swung at her again, but this time she parried the blade, and they began to trade sword strokes from their separate, bounding vehicles.

"You duel like a beginner," Spalko said in a taunting voice.

Flinging sweat from his brow with a rapid shake of his head, Mutt tried to get inside her blade, but she slipped away, her footing as sure as that of a gymnast on a balance beam.

Angered, Mutt stepped up onto the door and planted

his leading foot atop the rear fender of Spalko's jeep. But the two vehicles suddenly began to drift apart, leaving him wishboned between them and flailing his arms in the air.

Spalko laughed. "How I adore the minds of brash young men. So open. So quick to expend their energy."

She waited while the vehicles drew closer together before lunging at him. Mutt deflected the rapier, but the force of his parry carried him into the back of Spalko's jeep, and at the same time threw Spalko into the back of the duck. Spying the burlap sack, Mutt made a grab for it, but the driver of the jeep was already reaching for him, and the two of them ended up in a tussle, with the burlap bag changing hands several times before ending up clamped in Mutt's hand.

In the duck, Spalko sent the rapier through the back of the front seat, almost succeeding in impaling Marion on the blade. In answer, Marion slammed her foot down on the brake pedal, catapulting Spalko and her deadly blade clear out of the duck and onto the deck, where only her last-ditch grab for the front-mounted machine gun saved her from being run over.

And only by flattening herself to the seat was Marion saved from the machine gun's sudden hail of fire as it swung around, shredding what remained of the already shattered windshield. Yanking the steering wheel with both hands, as much in reaction to the machine gun as to rid herself of Spalko, she rammed the duck into the back of the jeep, sending Spalko sailing off the deck and into the jeep's front seat, where Mutt was wresting with the driver.

Spalko raised the rapier and feigned a twisting right-hand attack, then came at him underhanded. But he divined her intent at the last possible instant and deflected the blade. Parrying his lunge, she mounted a follow-up attack, but again he blocked her blade and counterattacked, their swords clanging a dozen times in half as many seconds.

"Well done," she said in genuine compliment. "But you're tiring quickly. You don't have the stamina to finish this."

Mutt knew she was right. Worse, rivulets of sweat were beginning to drip into his eyes, clouding his vision. Holding the burlap bag in one hand and summoning what strength he had left, he flicked the foil through a slashing downward stroke. Spalko slid out from under the attack, but the tip of the blade left a slice in the collar of her fatigues. Still, she might almost have planned it. Availing herself of Mutt's instant of wide-eyed surprise at having found an opening in her defense, she maneuvered the rapier straight down along his sword arm, opening a gash on his left cheek.

Wincing in pain, Mutt retreated to the rear of the jeep. Blood began to flow down his neck.

"Ah, your first wound," Spalko said, smiling. "I'm honored to have inflicted it."

When their swords crossed again, each of them put their weight behind the blades. "To win a fight like this, one needs balance," Spalko said when they were practically lip to lip. "Not force, not even expert skill with the blade, but *balance*."

She relaxed for an instant, then shoved with all her might, pushing Mutt out of the jeep and, at the same time, spearing the burlap sack with the rapier. Fortunately for Mutt, Indy had been watching the duel and came roaring up from the rear just as Mutt went airborne. Landing hard on the hood of Indy's truck, he scampered to his feet, shouting for Indy to catch up with Spalko.

Unfortunately for Mutt, the two vehicles were entering an area of thick forest, draped with vines and low-hanging limbs, and no sooner did Mutt turn to face front than one of the limbs caught him midsection and spun him up into the leafy canopy, while the jeep and the truck sprinted away.

Giving his head a clearing shake, Mutt found himself in the company of a dozen or so monkeys that were foraging for fruit. For a moment, the creatures simply stared at Mutt; then, screeching in surprise, the larger members of the troop began to pelt Mutt with twigs and whatever else was at hand, while the rest scampered into the higher branches, clasped their small paws and prehensile tails on vines, and fled. Not about to be left behind, Mutt reached out for what appeared to be the thickest vine, and let fly, swinging through the treetops like some leather-jacketed swashbuckler, monkeys to all sides of him.

Below, the two vehicles had twisted their way up a steep hillside and were now racing along the edge of a sheer cliff, several hundred feet above the river. Frustrated by the driver's caution, Spalko had taken the wheel and was closing fast on Indy's truck, bent on forcing it off the cliff. Mutt, however, was closing fast on Spalko's jeep. Riding one last vine to the very end of its long arc, he let go, dropping himself into the front seat, along with several monkeys that had apparently accepted him as their new troop leader. Knocked from the driver's seat by Mutt, Spalko lost sight of the burlap sack momentarily. When next she looked, the sack was in Mutt's hands, and he was leaping over the windshield into the back of Indy's truck.

Snatching the sack from Mutt, Oxley opened it in a rush, sighing contentedly when he saw that the crystal skull hadn't been damaged. But when Mutt looked to Indy for praise, all he got was a near smile and a "Not bad, kid."

Behind them — saved at the last instant by the quick-thinking soldier she had ordered out of the driver's seat — Spalko was on her feet in the front seat, cursing Indy in Russian and English. Taking aim at him, she hurled the rapier, only to watch as Mutt leaped into the path of the sword. But it was the crystal skull that ended up saving both of them. Raised overhead by Oxley in self-defense, the skull drew the blade to it magnetically and held it fast. Enraged, Spalko grabbed one of the monkeys that was scampering about inside the jeep and hurled it off the cliff.

Throwing all caution to the wind, Indy accelerated, widening the lead on Spalko's jeep. Up ahead, however, and completely blocking the trail, loomed an enormous mound of dirt. Indy's foot went to the brake pedal, but not soon enough. The truck bounded over a rotting log, went airborne, and came down hard on the side of the mound, stalling on impact. Not a moment later came Spalko's jeep, moving at an even faster clip, so that when it hit the log it sailed well over Indy and company, and crashed much closer to the summit of the mound.

Having braced herself for the collision, Spalko was in motion before the jeep stopped moving, drawing a pistol from the holster of one of the soldiers and aiming it down at Indy. But her finger had no sooner found the trigger than a huge ant scurried off the pistol's grip to sink its pincers into the soft flesh between her thumb and fore-finger. The pain of the bite tore a scream from Spalko's throat that seemed to summon a thousand more ants from the mound that was their nest, and they began to surge into the jeep through every air vent and hole in the floorboards. Below the jeep, thousands more were suddenly pouring from shafts in the mound itself.

In the front seat of the stalled truck, Mac yelled, "Bloody 'ell!"

"*Siafu* — army ants!" Indy said in the same panicked tone. "Everyone out!"

No one argued with him. Mac grabbed hold of Oxley — who had returned the skull to the burlap sack — and Indy grabbed hold of Mutt, and the four of them clambered from the truck and took off running down the face of the mound. Just then, though, the saw-blade-decapitated truck roared onto the scene, with Dovchenko at the wheel and, in the rear, a dozen soldiers he had picked up along the way. Hurling himself out the driver's-side door, the big Russian drove Indy to the ground, even as Indy was yelling for the others to make their way down to the river.

Oxley stumbled and fell, but momentum had Mac and Mutt in its grip and the two of them continued to barrel downhill. So, too, did the roofless truck, with the Russian soldiers in the rear beginning to take aim at the fugitives.

The first rounds missed their marks, however, and the follow-up fusillade never had a chance, intercepted as it was by the duck Marion placed neatly between the soldiers and their fleeing quarry.

Crouched down behind the steering wheel, Marion yelled for Mutt and Mac to hop aboard, stomped down on the gas pedal when they did, and aimed the duck lurching down toward the river. A hundred yards along, they came to a low cliff, where Marion was forced to bring the duck to a halt. Peering over the edge, she noted that the cliff was only thirty feet above the raging current, and that halfway down a large, leafy tree jutted out from the cliff face.

With clear purpose, she maneuvered the duck through a U-turn and started back up the incline.

CHAPTER TWENTY-ONE

On the slope of the army ant mound, Indy was taking a bruising. Either ignorant or indifferent to the river of ants streaming toward them, Dovchenko had Indy in his powerful grip and was choking the life out of him. The ants were seconds from swarming over both of them when Oxley suddenly appeared, pulling the crystal skull from the sack and holding it over his head as if it were a beacon.

Gleaming from the skull, shafts of reflected sunlight shone down on the river of ants, which immediately divided into two streams, leaving Indy, Dovchenko, and Oxley untouched on an island created by the split. By then Indy had managed to escape the Russian's hold, but he wasn't faring any better. Putting up his dukes, he threw a punch Dovchenko didn't even bother to block, simply took on the chin before grabbing Indy by the arm and flipping him judo-style to the ground.

Indy thought he would never get his wind back. When at last he staggered up to his feet, he saw Dovchenko charging straight at him. Whether Indy ducked at that moment or his wobbly legs refused to straighten, the result was the same: his head and right shoulder slammed into Dovchenko's midsection, and momentum carried the Russian through a front flip that landed him on his back in the center of the river of ants.

Thrilled to encounter the feast that had fallen into their midst, the ants immediately began to invade Dovchenko's mouth, ears, and nostrils, then to create entrances of their own by burrowing into his flesh. Dovchenko bellowed in a way Indy had never heard, and his last look of the Russian was a sight he would never forget: What had yet to be devoured was being moved horizontally to the ground by a writhing mass of ants, keen on carrying Dovchenko into their nest, where they could make a full meal out of him.

Also in flight from the ants, Spalko, along with the soldiers who had arrived in the truck, had been forced downhill to the low cliff that had thwarted Marion's attempt to reach the river, and was now rappelling over the edge of the cliff on ropes.

From the driver's seat of the duck, Marion spied Indy

racing for the river, carrying Oxley on his back. For whatever reason, the ants were not swarming them, but allowing
them to run safely in their midst. Steering into one of the
twin streams of ants, Marion maneuvered the duck close
enough for Indy to set Oxley down inside the vehicle and
throw himself aboard. Wiper blades flinging ants from the
windshield, Marion steered for the cliff she had seen
earlier.

"Uh, honey," Indy said when he realized where they
were headed, "you gotta stop this thing or we're going over
the edge."

"That's the idea," she told him.

Indy shook his head back and forth. "Bad idea! Give
me the wheel."

Showing Indy one of his own patented smiles, Marion
said, "Trust me."

The fact that Indy clamped his hands on the door
frame showed that he didn't, though Oxley seemed posi-
tively thrilled with the idea of going over the edge.

"Three times it drops," Indy heard him say. "Drop!
Drop! Drop!"

Then, all at once, the duck came to a jarring halt, not,
however, in the river but in the canopy of a tree that had
taken solid root on the side of the cliff. Indy didn't see any
more reason to trust Marion now than he did earlier. In
fact, given that Irina Spalko and several armed soldiers

were coming down the cliff on ropes, there seemed even *less* reason to trust her.

"We can't stay here," he thought to point out.

Marion glanced at him. "I don't plan to."

She began to tap the accelerator pedal, as if revving the engine. But the clutch was out and the duck was in gear, and the rear wheels were beginning to strain for purchase on the leafy limbs that were the only things keeping the duck from falling.

At the same time, the soldiers were getting closer, but now the duck was really rocking, surging forward and backwards in the treetop.

"The way down!" Oxley said, pointing to the river. "The way down!"

Pained screams began to ring out above them, echoing across the river, and suddenly it was raining army ants. The ants were leaping from the cliff like lemmings, and Mutt, Marion, Mac, and Oxley were back to slapping themselves and one another in an attempt to brush them away. But the added motion was all the duck needed to break free. Bending forward, the tree released the duck, then sprang back, flyswatting a few of the soldiers who had reached it.

The duck was airborne only for seconds before it struck the water prow-first, flattened out, and went spiraling into the center of the river, slaved to the raging current.

Marion got the vehicle under control, but when she smiled at Indy, he only grumbled.

"Way to go, Mom," Mutt said.

The rapids were getting worse by the moment, and Marion was forced to negotiate a stretch of dangerous water. The angled prow of the duck dropped down into one of the swirling holes, and water surged over the deck, soaking everyone. Mac flipped switches on the dashboard that activated the duck's propellers and the ride smoothed somewhat.

Indy took a moment to grin at Mutt. "You learn to fence like that in prep school?"

"Just one more useless talent," Mutt said.

"Not sure I'd call that one useless, kid."

"He was fencing champ two years in a row," Marion shouted, "but the school kicked him out for betting on the contests."

Indy's grin straightened. "Gambling? That's outrageous!"

"I bet on myself to win," Mutt explained. "I made a small fortune."

Mac swung around to give Mutt a solid clap on the back. "Atta boy!"

Indy shot him a look. "Hey, do you mind? I'm trying to be a good parent here."

Mac made light of it. "Nothing wrong with the kid

taking a little action. It shows initiative." Again he swung to Mutt. "Just remember to cover the downside in case you're ever forced to throw a match."

Marion was doing all she could to avoid the eddies and whirlpools, but it was becoming obvious that the river had them, and it was going to do what it wanted with them.

The front of the duck went under again, and water flooded into the passenger compartment. Mutt screamed in pain and began waving his hand about. A rainbow-bellied fish had clamped itself onto his forefinger.

"Piranha," Indy said matter-of-factly.

Mutt screamed louder and Marion joined in. And she continued screaming even after Mutt had shaken the fish loose.

"It's all right, Mom," he started to say, until he realized what she and now Indy and Mac were screaming at.

"Falls!" everyone said in unison.

Marion raised herself up in the driver's seat. "Hold on!"

"Down . . ." Oxley said.

The duck nosedived and landed hard, bobbing like a cork at the foot of the falls before continuing down-river. Water gushed into the passenger cabin, filling it like a kiddy pool. But everyone had managed to remain inside.

"Well, Ox, you wanted us in the river," Indy said, sluicing water from his face.

Indy looked past him to the shoreline, where Spalko and her troops were hurrying down a path that paralleled the river. He blew his breath out in exasperation. "The way down isn't *in* the river, it's alongside it."

But Oxley only nodded to something in the distance. "Down."

"Falls!" Marion screamed again.

The first nosedive turned out to be a mere practice run for the rapids and second waterfall they were swept into. The screaming and the freefall lasted longer, and the landing was rougher by far. The duck emerged from the spray with everyone gasping for air. And the worst was still ahead of them, in the form of a third waterfall that made the first two look like trickles.

"Three times it falls!" Marion said, gesturing to the falls.

While Indy was considering it, Oxley said, "Oh, down . . . *three times* it drops!"

There was simply no way to keep the duck upright. The stern came around, and everyone was tossed into open space. The duck crumpled on hitting the water and inverted. And for a long moment, there was nothing but the frothing water and mist. Then, a quarter mile downriver, where the current became gentle, five heads broke the surface, and one by one Indy and the rest dragged themselves up onto a sandy bank.

Indy gazed around him. The river had deposited them in an area of towering mesas clad in thick primary forest. It was as if they had traveled back in time.

Indy crawled over to Marion, put an arm under her shoulders, and turned her toward him. Like everyone else, she had swallowed a lot of water and was bruised from the fall, but he knew she was tough as nails and would be all right. Still, he was so relieved, he gathered her in his arms and held her tightly for several seconds.

Easing out of his impulsive embrace, she looked into his eyes. "Not getting tired, are you, Jones?" she teased.

He grinned. "Baby, you got no idea."

"Sure I do. The way you live, running off on adventures to every corner of the world and back again?"

Indy laughed shortly. "It ain't the mileage, honey. It's the years."

Seated on his haunches nearby, Mutt turned away from the loving couple, and Mac loosed a snort of dismissal.

A sudden rustling in the branches behind Mutt made him turn around. Oxley emerged from the jungle like a robot. He had removed the crystal skull from the burlap bag, and now placed it on the beach, rotating it to face the mesa behind them.

Mutt thought his ears were ringing from having been underwater, and he tipped his head from side to side to empty them. But, in fact, the sound he heard was emanating from the skull, which was also vibrating, causing beach pebbles to leap about.

Indy left Marion's side to join Oxley. Following his rapt gaze, he realized that the forested cliff behind them was carved in the representation of a giant head, a horse-tail of water cascading from the face's left eye socket.

"Akator?" Mutt said.

"We've found it!" Indy exclaimed.

"*Through eyes that last I saw in tears,*'" Oxley said.

"Now I remember!" Mutt said suddenly. He swung to Indy. "When Ox kept repeating that at the Russians' camp, I knew I'd heard it before. It's from a poem Ox made me memorize when I was like ten years old. By T.S. Eliot, I think." He stopped to gather his thoughts. "*Through eyes that last I saw in tears; the golden vision reappears. Through eyes that last I saw in tears, here in death's dream kingdom, the golden vision reappears.*'"

"*Golden* vision?" Mac said in sudden interest. "I'm in."

Mutt stood up to get a better vantage on the great stone face, identical to that of the crystal skull. "Through eyes in *tears*! That's the entrance — through the waterfall."

Indy's glance held admiration. Then he looked at the carved cliff face. "We're going up there. The skull has to be returned."

"Returned?" Marion said.

Mutt glanced at the stone face once more. "Without any climbing gear? Are you crazy?"

"You don't have to come," Indy said, getting to his feet and clapping sand from his hands. "But the skull has to be returned."

Mutt stared at him. "You see what it did to Ox. Why does it have to be returned?"

"Why you?" Marion asked.

Indy hesitated. "Well, because it asked me to."

Marion's eyes searched his face. "Jones . . ."

Mutt looked from one to the other. "It asked you to? A hunk of dead rock?"

Indy prepared to set off for the cliff. "What makes you think it's dead?"

CHAPTER TWENTY-TWO

For all the wounds and bruises, sword slashes, ant bites, punches, and slaps they had suffered, their excitement at arriving at the lost city energized them for the tricky ascent. What were a few aches and pains, after all, when ancient wonders waited?

And, perhaps, untold wealth as well.

The burlap sack hitched to his pants, Oxley led the way up the steep face, angling for the waterfall that spilled from the left eye. Indy and the rest were strung out behind. Hand- and footholds were abundant, but it was slow going nonetheless.

Despite Oxley's admonitions, Indy had searched for an entrance lower in the cliff face — in the mouth and nose — but the openings had proved to be dead ends. It stood to reason that there were other, easier ways to reach the top of the mesa, but those could take days to search out, and they didn't have days. The jungle could provide them with water, fruits, and fish, but at some point they were going to have to follow the Sono upriver to the road and return to Iquitos. Alternatively they could follow the river to its confluence with the Amazon, in the hope of encountering villages there. But either way, they were in for a long and difficult journey.

Marion was ahead of Indy as they began their traverse toward the waterfall. She was climbing well, when all at once an outcropping crumbled under her fingertips and she began to belly-slide down the face, screaming Indy's name. Wrapping his arm about a stout tree trunk, Indy leaned out as far as he could, just managing to catch her as she slid past, and hoist her even with him.

"Twice in one day," she said. "I'm flattered."

Indy grinned. "Plenty more waiting."

He resumed the ascent, moving more quickly now, eagerness spurring him on, even when the rock grew slippery under his hands. The dark arch of the eye was above him, and just to his left the heavy plume of rushing water. Through the mist he watched Oxley enter the cascade and vanish into the rock. Following Oxley's route, Indy scampered to the left as he came alongside the corner of the eye. Swaying precariously in the force of the falls, he threw himself into the eye, behind which was a tunnel that served as a channel for the water.

Behind him, he heard Marion call to him again. Extending his arm down into the cascade, he found her hand and pulled her into the tunnel. Then he did the same for Mutt.

"Just like fishing," Indy said.

Reaching into the waterfall a third time, he yanked Mac through the eye and into the relatively calm water. From deeper in the tunnel they heard Oxley cry for them to hurry, and when they looked they could see him silhouetted against a circle of light, a good distance away.

Indy started to hurry toward him, but stopped when he realized that the walls of the tunnel were covered in painted panels of stunning beauty. Indy's breath caught in his throat. The Minoan murals of Knossos and the Mayan murals of Bonampak paled by comparison. They had discovered a wonder of the ancient world.

Gingerly, Indy touched the first panel, which depicted a group of squatting human figures, their hands extended above their heads, as if to the sun. He rubbed his fingertips together. "Ochre . . . charcoal . . . iron oxide . . ." The tunnel wall itself was studded with sconces, above which were smears of black residue too fresh to have been deposited centuries earlier.

"How old do you think these paintings are?" Mac asked while Indy was gazing about in sudden wariness.

"Mesolithic, possibly. Six, eight thousand years."

Mac looked dubious. "South America wasn't even inhabited by humans that long ago."

"Nonsense," Indy said.

They moved to the next panel, which showed the same group of humans gazing at a tall, glowing, vaguely humanoid figure that was descending from the sky.

"Someone arrived," Indy said.

Mutt studied the humanoid figure. "Who?"

"Good question. But many of the pre-Columbian cultures have legends of godlike beings arriving, with superior knowledge of medicine, weaving, agriculture, writing, and astronomy. Kukulkan, Quetzalcoatl, beings from Egypt or Atlantis, take your pick. They were the equivalent of our belief in flying saucer people, arriving from space to save us from ourselves."

"Save us?" Mutt said skeptically. "Not in the movies I've seen about spacemen."

Indy snorted. "That's because those movies aren't really about beings from outer space. They're about paranoia."

They moved deeper into the tunnel, stopping at a panel showing a dozen more humanoid figures intermingling with the humans, building, farming, healing the sick.

"Whoever they were," Indy said, "they taught the Ugha how to work with stone, irrigate the fields, cure illnesses."

The next painting was a more detailed representation of one of the visitors in profile. Indy's fingertip traced the elongated head depicted in the painting. It matched the shape of the crystal skull precisely.

No one spoke until they had arrived at the next painting, which showed the thirteen humanoids grouped in a circle.

Glancing at other panels, Indy said, "They're always depicted as a group, in a circle." He indicated two neighboring panels. "There. And there."

They entered a chamber that was darker than most, but larger as well, and adorned with immense paintings. In one the Ugha were engaged in battle with invaders wearing breastplates and pointed helmets, and carrying muskets and powder horns.

"The conquistadors," Mutt said. "Searching for El Dorado."

"Finding El Dorado," Indy amended.

Huge wall panels showed the Ugha fighting valiantly with spears, and with what looked like whirling helicopter blades. Others revealed their utter defeat. In the final panel, one of the thirteen humanoid figures was headless, and his skull was being carried off by the invaders.

"No gold," Indy remarked. "Just the head — the skull."

"And a chest filled with bronze coins," Mutt added.

Indy grinned at him. "Good thinking."

In an adjoining room, they came to a panel in which the thirteen humanoids were dying, decaying.

Mutt regarded it. "Why didn't the other twelve just leave?"

Indy glanced at the light at the end of the tunnel. "Maybe we'll find out."

The final chamber was a rotunda, with thirteen bas-relief skulls decorating the upper portion of the walls, each of them six feet tall. Indy and the others were passing beneath them when the skulls began to shudder, raining plaster on everyone, then explode.

CHAPTER TWENTY-THREE

*I*rina Spalko and the few soldiers who had bushwhacked their way down the Sono River regarded the wreckage of the duck, which had washed up onto the same small beach Indy and the others had occupied. The Russians were exhausted. What Jones hadn't done to them, ants, spiders, hornets, and thorns had. But Spalko's sudden fall to her knees in the sand owed nothing to fatigue, and everything to her sixth sense.

"They've found it!" she said. "They've found Akator."

Just then a soldier emerged from the foliage and pressed a blinking diode into her hand.

"Where did you find it?" she said.

Leading her a few steps into the treeline, he parted two giant fronds and pointed to the cliff that overshadowed the beach. Spalko gazed up at the enormous face the ancients had carved into the limestone, and she managed a smile.

They had found Akator, and now she had as well.

*   *   *

The skull sculptures had given birth to a band of Ugha warriors. Powerfully built, they wore their long hair in top-knots, or bizarre arrangements that suggested animal horns or crowns. Their teeth were filed to points and their faces were lightened with ash and clay. Jaguar claws and peccary tusks dangled from their necklaces, and their distended earlobes dropped nearly to the tops of their shoulders. They were armed with stone knives and short spears, but their weapon of choice was the three-balled bola, one of which had Mutt's name on it. Catching him before he could react, the whirling weapon wrapped itself around his neck, almost crushing his skull and slamming him to the floor of the rotunda.

In a flash, Indy was kneeling beside him, uncoiling the bola and helping him to his feet, even as warriors continued to crash through the remains of the skull masks, issuing war cries that echoed through the contiguous chambers. Mac fled for the end of the tunnel, with Marion, Indy, and Mutt hot on his heels.

Oxley was already outside the tunnel, standing on a platform at the top of a long stairway that wound down into Akator. The ruins of civic buildings, temples, and towering stelae occupied the whole of a craterlike depression in the mesa's flat top. Rugged hills encircled the crater and were themselves rimmed by clouds. The largest of the hills had been hollowed by hand and nature to catch the rain and serve as Akator's reservoir, from which descended a system of aqueducts that channeled water to all parts of the plateau. Though thick forest had reclaimed most of the city, blanketing the slopes and much of the flat land, it was still possible to discern the design of Akator, whose broad avenues radiated from a tiered, central pyramid of grand stairways, flanked by immense carvings of snake heads.

Oxley was enraptured. From the first moment he had set foot in Akator he felt as if he had come home, and now that same feeling took hold of him. But his blissful state was short-lived. Behind him, mayhem spilled from the tunnel in the form of Indy and the others, pursued by a dozen shrieking, near-naked warriors armed with bolas.

Leading the retreat, Oxley began to race down the flight of stairs, but more Ugha were waiting at the foot of the staircase. Last in line, Indy was slammed to the plaza's hard paving stones by two warriors. Hissing in rage, they were close to wrapping their bolas around his neck when Mutt drove both of them off Indy with a headfirst dive.

Indy was about to thank him when Marion issued a cry for help. A warrior had leaped on her back and was tearing at her hair. Indy's bullwhip lashed out, catching the Ugha around the neck. A snap of Indy's arm yanked the warrior off Marion and sent him sprawling into a stone wall. Elsewhere, Mac was battling it out with three Ugha, throwing nonstop punches, elbows, and kicks, and holding his own. But with every passing minute, more warriors were appearing.

Realizing the hopelessness of the situation, Indy shouted to Oxley. "How did you get past them? What do we do?"

Oxley glanced at him, but in a distracted way.

"Harold! We're going to die!"

Oxley seemed to comprehend, but he remained non-chalant as he opened the burlap sack, removed the skull, and held it high over his head. Captured and refracted sunlight streamed not merely from the skull's huge eyes but from its ears, nasal openings, and mouth as well. And as had happened on the beach, the skull emitted a low hum and began to vibrate wildly — actually *blur* — in Oxley's grip.

To a man, the warriors froze in their tracks and fell silent, staring at the skull in terrified fascination and drop-ping to their knees in reverence. When Oxley began to back away in the direction of the central pyramid, Indy spurred everyone into motion and grabbed hold of Oxley to hurry him along. Watching them, the Ugha began to shrink back, as if afraid to follow.

"Do we go up?" Indy asked when they reached the foot of the pyramid's snake-flanked staircase.

"Up," Oxley said. "Up."

The steep climb was made more difficult by the narrowness of the stair treads and the disproportionate height of the risers separating them. Halfway to the summit, Indy stopped to gaze around, his eyes wide and his pulse quick. In Akator's architecture he saw hints of all that had followed in the Americas: the massive monolithic structures of Tihuanaco and Sacsahuaman, the precision stonework of Machu Picchu, the animal-head sculpture of Chavin, the lofty, corbel arch temples of Tikal and Chichen Itza, the elaborate and sometimes ghoulish carvings of Tenochtitlan ... Akator was America's Atlantis — *proto*-city from which all others had evolved.

Ultimately they reached the structure's flat top, where, in lieu of the temple Indy expected to find, was a large square basin filled with sand. Plunged into the sand were four enormous triangular-shaped obelisks, lying on their sides with their bases touching. The obelisks appeared to have once formed a single obelisk that had been cleaved into four identical parts. Their distal ends were supported on squat stone pillars located at the four corners of the structure's roof.

Indy glanced at Oxley, who gave his head a perplexed shake.

"Oxley made it this far," he told the others, "but he couldn't figure out where to leave the skull."

Hanging on Indy's every word, Oxley said, "*To lay their just hands on that Golden Key that opes the Palace of Eternity ...*'"

"Those lines from Milton again," Indy said. His eyes went from Oxley to the obelisks and back to Oxley. "The key?" He gestured to the lengths of carved stone. "These four parts form the key that ... opens the Palace of Eternity?"

Oxley's stare held affirmation.

Indy stepped back to study the obelisks. "It's a puzzle. We have to reassemble the original obelisk."

Mac laughed in disbelief. "Mate, these things have to weigh four tons apiece."

Circling the basin, Indy noticed a trickle of sand that had leaked from around the edges of a wooden plug in one of the retaining walls and that the plug was merely one of a series of such plugs set into each of the basin's four walls. Moving to the nearest stone pillar, Indy began to search the area, though for what he didn't say.

Watching him, Mac said, "So this is El Dorado, eh? A pile of rubble." In disgust, he kicked at the sand that had caught Indy's eye. "Where's all the bloody gold? What kind of legend is —"

Indy whirled suddenly, holding a huge stone over his head. Roaring with effort, he raced toward Mac, who leaped out of the way in the nick of time. However, the rock he thought was meant for him slammed down on the wooden plug in the basin wall, knocking it from its hole and allowing a thick stream of sand to flow from the basin.

"Trying to brain me, mate?" Mac said.

He might have said more, but just then a grating sound filled the air, and the distal ends of the obelisks began to rise ever so slightly from the pillars that supported them. His face lit up in sudden revelation, Mac located a stone and brought it down on one of the other plugs. As more sand flowed from the basin, the obelisk parts levitated again, their bases moving closer together and their ends edging ever so slowly toward vertical. Mutt joined in, and the three of them began to move methodically from plug to plug. Sand spilled out to coat the flat roof and the obelisks continued to rise and fuse into one column.

Watching from the sidelines, Marion smiled at seeing father and son working together, and marveled at the sight of fifteen tons of stone being reunited, aided only by gravity and the ingenuity of Akator's builders.

In the end, they resorted to scooping sand out of the basin with their hands to hurry the process. Then, finally, the obelisk bases slid into place on the last remaining grains of sand, and the four pieces came fully to vertical with a resounding *thud!*

Stepping back to appreciate their handiwork, Indy was about to say, "Now what?" when the floor of the basin began to rumble and groan, then iris open, revealing a vast conical inner chamber of the tiered pyramid. More, the reassembled obelisk proved to be only the tip of a still-larger obelisk that rose one hundred feet from the inner floor of the structure.

That alone would have provided enough excitement for one day, but suddenly the entire roof of the building was opening — pocking itself into grooves engineered into the edges of the platform — the basin walls separating, sand cascading down into the dimly lit chamber, and Indy and the others searching desperately for something to hold on to.

Backing to the edge of what had been roof only moments earlier, they realized that a narrow walkway spiraled down the circumference of the obelisk. Leaping onto the walkway, they initially began to pick their way toward the floor, then hurry toward it, as the walkway, too, began to retract into the obelisk, leaving all of them hanging by their fingertips, thirty feet from hard floor.

In someone's footprints in the sand that dusted the tops of the disappearing stairs, a diode flashed, as if in an urgent plea for help. Brushed from the edge of the tread as the stair retracted fully, the small electronic transmitter plummeted into the darkness.

Standing at the top on the stone steps that led down into the lost city, Irina Spalko took a moment to regard the tracking diode flashing in the palm of her hand. Beside her stood two soldiers, wisps of smoke issuing from the barrels of their automatic weapons, and below her sprawled the bullet-ridden bodies of dozens of Ugha warriors.

Spalko handed the blinking diode to one of the soldiers, who dropped it into a box containing several more just like it.

"*Poidyomte*," she said, gesturing to the central pyramid, and the three of them set off down the stairs.

Chapter TWENTY-FOUR

*M*arion was the last to let go of the withdrawing spiral stairway. A scream accompanied her fall, but instead of the painful landing she imagined she found herself in the comfort of Indy's arms.

He grinned as he set her on her feet. "I hear the third time's a charm."

She smiled with her eyes. "We'll see, Jones. We'll see."

Intricately carved statuary and bas-relief wall panels covered nearly every square inch of the lower reaches of the pyramid's inner chamber. Even the hundred-foot-tall obelisk was covered with glyphs and symbols. Still, for all the carving, the interior felt more like a cave system than the interior of a pyramid, right down to the branching roots of trees that had penetrated the shell. With nothing to indicate where the skull should be left, Indy decided to explore one of the corridors that radiated from the chamber. That meant leaving behind the sunlight that entered the chamber from above, but Indy didn't see that they had much choice. As his eyes began to adjust to the darkness, he saw that water had been channeled into the interior and put to good use in powering the rotation of dozens of stone wheels, ten feet in diameter.

"Turbines," Indy said. Holding his hand above a metal conduit that ran from one of the wheels, he felt a faint charge in the air. "Electrical conductors. The . . . legends told of these."

Continuing down the corridor, they came to a series of fixtures that began to glow as they passed, providing a diffuse, greenish light. Indy hoisted himself up onto a column base to observe the fixtures more closely. From one, a green liquid had leaked through cracks in the fixture's glasslike cover. He touched his hand to the liquid and peered at it.

"Light emitting," he said in awe.

The fixtures tracked their movements, glowing as Indy and the rest approached, fading in as they moved away. The deeper they went, the more intricate and opulent the carvings and adornments. In one room they found the walls hung with plaques of pure silver, inset with garnets, opals, jade, and other precious stones.

"Now this is more like it," Mac said. Surreptitiously, he began to stuff his pockets with stones chipped from the plaques.

Behind Mac, Mutt spotted a jewel-encrusted representation of the sun sitting on a stone shelf. He had just picked it up when Marion slapped him on the wrist. He responded to her disapproving scowl with his most innocent expression.

"I wasn't going to keep it, you know."

Replacing the piece, he hurried to catch up with Indy. But without a mom to reprimand him, Mac snatched and pocketed the sun.

His eyes searching the dimness for signs of a throne room, Indy led everyone through a sharp turn in the corridor. But what he saw next made him freeze in his tracks. The room was filled with corpses: placed in a circle and sitting upright in lifelike poses. Moving to one of them, Indy saw that the corpse's skull was charred around the eye sockets.

Mutt swallowed hard. "They're burned, all of them. What happened here?"

"Another good question," Indy said.

While Indy was shaking his head in ignorance, Mac rid some of the corpses of bracelets and rings, then tried to find space for them in his already-bulging pockets.

Four feet from the floor, recesses of various sizes hollowed the walls of the room, each containing a statue or totem or piece of pottery. At first, Indy couldn't believe his eyes, but the more he looked, the more he grasped that the antiquities dated to nearly every era of humankind.

"Prehistoric, Mesolithic," he said, beginning to identify the contents of the niches. "Babylonian, Sumerian, Egyptian . . . This place is the mother lode!" It was clear now where the Chauchilla Cemetery's chest of bronze coins had originated.

Mac was all but salivating. "There isn't a museum anywhere that wouldn't sell its soul for this. A dozen museums, a hundred . . ."

Indy stopped to drink it all in. "The beings the Ugha regarded as gods . . . they were archaeologists."

Two enormous doors dominated the far wall of the room. As Indy and Oxley approached, slivers of iron ore began to whisk from the walls and the floor and cling to the crystal skull like strands of hair. By the time Oxley reached the doors, the skull appeared to have been given flesh and a semblance of face.

Mutt ran his hands over the doors. "How do we open them?"

Indy searched the room for clues. The niches that adorned the walls were located at uniform height, but above the doors, perhaps seven feet from the floor, was an empty recess.

"Whatever's behind these doors was reserved for the

true builders of the city — the gods. And by the looks of things, they were tall." Turning, he tried to take the crystal skull from Oxley, but Oxley drew away from him. "I'll give it back, Ox," Indy said. "Promise."

Reluctantly, Oxley loosened his hold on the skull and surrendered it to Indy, who immediately swung to Mutt.

"Give me a boost," he said, nodding his chin toward the niche above the doors.

Mutt fashioned a stirrup with his interlocked hands. Indy planted his right foot, and Mutt pushed him into the air. At the apex of his ascent, Indy shoved the crystal skull into the recess and felt it click into place, almost as if the skull had been molded from the niche itself.

Immediately, the skull began to glow, brighter than any of them had seen it glow, and the metal shavings it had attracted erupted into the air. The doors issued a deep groan and began to chevron open. Repelled from each other like the opposing poles of magnets, they pocketed themselves in the walls, revealing the pyramid's *sanctum sanctorum* — the throne room.

Still poised in Mutt's stirrup, Indy pulled the skull from the recess and hopped down to the floor. Handing the skull to Oxley, he crossed the threshold, entering a room of such blinding radiance he was forced to shield his eyes with his hands. Circular, the room was constructed of stone, in the style of the ancient builders of South

America, though the ceiling was so high it was lost in darkness. Offerings littered the floor and filled every niche in the walls. But the real evidence that they had finally arrived at their destination sat atop the room's concentric altar, in the form of a baker's dozen of tall enthroned figures.

"No more forever waiting soon now," Oxley said, speaking softly to the skull.

Mutt pivoted through a slow circle, regarding the silent seated figures, his gaze resting on one that lacked a skull. "Let me guess: the skull's his."

With Mutt and Marion looking on in wonder, Oxley began to draw near the headless figure. Indy had just stepped to one side when he heard a familiar *click!* Turning, he saw that Mac had drawn his pistol and was aiming it at everyone in a general way.

"Sorry, Indy," he said.

For a moment, Indy was more annoyed than angry. "Will you make up your mind?"

Marion blew out her breath. "I'm getting really tired of this guy."

Mac glanced from Marion to Indy. "I warned you not to bet on me, mate." Out of the corner of his mouth, he yelled, "*Ya evo poimal.*"

And Irina Spalko and three Russian soldiers entered the throne room.

Indy shot Mac a look of incredulity. "You're a *triple* agent?"

"Nah," Mac said. "I just lied about being a double." Eyeing Marion, he added, "Don't worry, honey. You can come with us."

She laughed in his face. "Fat chance."

Gently, Spalko lifted the crystal skull from Oxley's hands and regarded it pensively. "Now," she said. "Speak to me now."

"It won't," Indy interrupted. "You're like the conquistadors, looking for gold. These beings weren't conquerors. They brought knowledge. They were teachers. That's why the skull spoke to Oxley and me."

Spalko either didn't hear him, or chose not to. When next she fixed her gaze on the skull, something changed: the crystal eyes began to glow.

A light came into Spalko's eyes as well. "Look at them," she said, gesturing broadly to the thirteen beings. "For seven thousand years they have waited for the return of the one taken from them. They are a hive mind — one being, physically separate but with a collective consciousness. More powerful together than they could ever be apart." Holding the skull in both hands, she advanced on the headless figure. "Imagine what they'll be able to tell us."

"I can't," Indy said. "Neither could the people who were instructed to build this temple and neither can you."

"*Belief,* Dr. Jones," she said, without bothering to look at him. "It is a gift you have yet to receive. My sympathies."

"Oh, I believe, sister . . ." Indy said.

Spalko had reached the foot of the altar stairs when an unseen forced wrenched the skull from her hands and drew it into position atop the shoulders of the figure.

". . . that's why I'm staying down here," Indy finished.

For a moment, a thick silence descended on the throne room. Then alien sounds began to rise from the formerly headless one. Only when the rest replied in kind did Indy accept that the thirteen were conversing. They hadn't exchanged much when a deep sound emanated from somewhere deep below the chamber, and the circular wall began to shudder. Carvings splintered and cracked, and totems vibrated from the niches and smashed on the stone floor.

Spalko, Mac, and the Russian soldiers looked around the room in sudden concern as the shaking reached a crescendo. Masonry and stucco began to crumble, and the stones that formed the perimeter wall collapsed, exposing an entirely different surface, perhaps metal, perhaps something that had never been glimpsed by human eyes.

The rumbling continued to increase in volume and intensity, and the thirteen seated beings began to shudder in sympathy, losing their earthly garments to reveal beings of flawless crystal.

Fluids began to course through their bodies, and flesh of a kind began to mantle their crystalline bodies.

They were coming to life.

Without warning, Oxley began to mutter in what sounded like a precursor to Quechua.

Cautiously, Indy raised his eyes to the restored figure, which placed the palms of its hands together to form an X and gave them a downward twist. Indy looked back at Oxley, who was talking faster and more urgently.

"What does he say?" Spalko demanded.

"He says he's grateful. He wants . . . he means the skeleton wants to give us a gift. A big gift."

Spalko glanced from Oxley to the aliens. "Tell me everything you know! I want it all. I want to know. . . ."

As the thirteen swung to her, Mutt rushed forward in excitement, only to be restrained by Indy. "Hang on, genius."

The bodies took on additional flesh, and the eyes of all thirteen began to glow, brighter than those of the original skull, and with what Indy felt was *ferocity*.

"Their *eyes*," Marion gasped.

"I've got a bad feeling about this," Indy said, retreating a step.

"Indy, aren't you going to look?" Marion asked.

"I found what I was looking for," Indy said, and flashed Marion a quick grin.

Mutt looked at them. "What is it? What are they, spacemen?"

"Interdimensional beings, in point of fact," Oxley said suddenly.

Indy swung to him and smiled. "Welcome back, Ox."

Then, all at once, the curved wall of the throne room shed the last of its stone trappings and began to spin, slowly at first, but quickly accruing velocity, like a centrifuge warming up. Born of thin air, a whirlpool formed in the center of the floor, enlarging as everyone watched, and sucking into it some of the debris that had piled up.

"What the heck is that thing?!" Marion said, clutching on to Indy's arm.

"A singularity," Oxley said flatly. "A portal. A pathway."

"A problem!" Indy chimed in.

With a nod toward the doorway, he turned and raced from the throne room, Mutt and Marion steps behind him and dragging Oxley with them. In seconds the four of them were tearing through the antechamber, where some of the corpses pulverized in their wake.

"Multiple dimensions," Oxley was saying. "What a concept! *Fascinating* to ponder. Mignon Thorne wrote an interesting perspective teased out of the notion of changeable physics."

"Not the best time for this, Ox," Indy shouted over his shoulder.

The corridor was shaking so hard they could scarcely stay on their feet. But at least they had arrived at the water-driven turbines, which meant that the central chamber was within reach. In an instant, though, several of the stone turbines toppled from their bases and began to roll toward them, shattering the aqueducts and loosing a flood.

CHAPTER TWENTY-FIVE

Mac and the three Russian soldiers weren't sure what to do. Spalko had moved dangerously close to the leading edge of the singularity and was locking gazes with each of the thirteen beings in turn. But the revolving wall had picked up speed and was suddenly yanking wristwatches, belt buckles, guns, and cartridges to the whirling perimeter. In reflexive self-defense, Spalko drew her rapier, only to watch it shoot from her hands and fly completely through one of the soldiers before wedding itself to the spinning wall.

Run through by the sword, the soldier dropped to his knees, then to the floor, dead.

Spalko stood motionless, caught in the concentrated glow of the crystal eyes. Her body stiffened, and she lifted her gaze to the altar.

"I can see! I can see it all!"

What Mac saw was a bad deal coming. Pivoting, he dashed from the throne room.

Evading the rolling turbines, Indy and the others doubled back and hurried into a secondary corridor, hoping that it would lead eventually to the central obelisk. With the aqueducts collapsed, the passageways were rapidly filling with water.

"A bit like eddies in water, but with hot and cold spots," Oxley said as he sloshed through the rising water alongside Indy. "You see what I'm on about? Post-inflation bubbles, Thorne calls them, assuming universal expansion, and therefore random pockets of extrinsic physics, where different realities can reside in the same space at the same time, completely unaware of one another."

Behind them, Indy heard someone call his name. Coming to a sudden halt, he turned to see Mac galloping through the surging water.

"Hold up, mate. I'm on your side, remember?"

In the throne room, the two remaining soldiers were edging toward the doorway. Zigzagging fissures had opened areas of the floor and the circular altar. The Russians were just short of the threshold when the lead soldier made inadvertent eye contact with one of the crystal beings. Paralyzed, he tried to shut his eyes but couldn't. Blood began to flow from his eye sockets, and he collapsed to the floor, hands pressed to the sides of his head in agony. Behind him, the second soldier raised his gaze for a split second and was similarly impaled on the gaze of another of the humanoids.

The sides of the room a blur now, Spalko tried desperately to look away. But quicker than seemed possible, the beings had left the altar to surround her, so that no matter where she turned she found herself trapped in the lethal glow of a pair of eyes.

"Cover them!" she yelled. "Cover them!"

But no one heard her plea.

Held fast in the gaze of the beings, she began to babble in their unearthly language, then scream in anguish as the knowledge she had sought for so long poured into her, unfiltered. The veins in her temples pulsed and swelled, and blood began to drip from her eyes.

"I can see everything!" she shrieked.

Somehow she remained on her feet, swaying back and forth but rooted in place. Smoke drifted from her eyes, her eyeballs bobbing about in their sockets as if being boiled by her brain. Geysers of flame burst from her eyes, and molten matter began to run down her face. Eye sockets blackened like those of the corpses in the antechamber, she exhaled for the last time. Then her arms dropped lifelessly to her sides, and she crumpled to the floor.

At the same time, the thirteen crystal beings began to vanish, one by one, turning sideways and slipping away, as if into another dimension.

Simultaneous with their leave-taking, the singularity began to swell, filling the room, then spilling into the antechamber and the pyramid's radiating passageways.

Mac clapped Indy on the back while water rose to their knees. "Well, we did it, mate."

Indy's stare mixed rage and disbelief. "You've gotta be kidding me."

Mac adopted a look of confusion. "What? You knew I was with you all the time, right?"

Indy firmed his lips and gave his head a shake. "It's whoever's in the room, isn't it, Mac." He blew out his breath and gestured forward. "All right. Come on."

They began to run, catching up with Mutt, Marion, and Oxley just as they were entering the central chamber. Hearing Mac slip and fall, Indy brought himself to a skidding halt and swung around.

"Can't move, mate," Mac said, his head just above water. "That thing's got me."

Farther down the corridor, the leading edge of the singularity was advancing on Mac, drawing everything into it, including the bracelets, rings, and other items Mac had pilfered and were now being drawn from his pockets.

"Come on, Indy," Mac said, showing him a rueful look. "You can't blame a guy for trying."

Indy's eyes widened, but he stayed put. "Get rid of all of it, Mac! Get rid of the metal!"

Nipping at Mac's drenched clothing, the singularity fastened Mac to the floor. Struggling for breath, he rolled over onto his back, coughing, gasping, kicking, and continuing to rid himself of the loot he carried. But the sinkhole had him now, and he was beginning to slide down the corridor toward it. At Mac's final appeal for help, Indy overcame his own fear and made a desperate leap for him, just managing to grab hold of Mac's wet hands. For a moment — his right arm wrapped around a pillar for leverage — Indy thought he would be able to drag Mac forward, but he soon realized that Mac was in danger of being torn in half.

"No way out of this one, mate," Mac said in a resigned voice. "You gotta let me go, Indy."

Indy tried to put a cheerful face on it. "Come on, Mac. We've been through worse than this."

Mac shook his head. "Not this time."

Wrenching his hands free, Mac surrendered to the force and was immediately sucked screaming into the expanding void.

Indy squeezed his eyes shut. He might have remained there had Marion and Mutt not called to him.

Getting to his feet, he scrambled forward. By then, the others had reached the base of the towering obelisk, but what with the spiral walkway still retracted, there appeared to be no way to escape the singularity.

With a deafening *crack!* the walls of the chamber split open and more water began to surge in from all sides. Soaked to the skin, Indy and the others dashed to the other side of the obelisk, where they discovered an inclined tunnel made of some quartzlike material that had yet to fill with water. Daylight brightened the distal end of the tunnel, but it seemed a long way off. Regardless, they scurried inside and tried their best to scramble upward, undermined by the tunnel's slick floor and steepness.

Marion, out in front, yelled back: "Move it, Jones!"

"You're the boss."

They weren't halfway to the light when the rising water overtook them and propelled them upward, ultimately hurling them onto a grassy slope some distance from the central pyramid, close to the carved cliff face they had ascended.

Below, Akator's central structure was collapsing, and

everything that wasn't nailed down was cycloning in the air. The four survivors were running for higher ground when the pyramid imploded with a thunderous sound, devastating most of the city's main plaza. A metallic orb appeared at the center of the maelstrom, surrounded by a debris cloud almost as wide as the ceremonial center itself. Then, turning sideways, the orb simply vanished from sight, dispersing the debris to all quarters of the mesa.

With its aqueducts and supports undermined, the earthen walls that contained the reservoir avalanched, and countless gallons of water began to flood the entire city, creating a mountain lake where Akator had stood.

"Like a broom to their footprints," Oxley said as the churning waters were beginning to subside.

No one spoke for several minutes. Dusk descended on the jungle and stars began to appear in the velvet sky.

Indy broke the silence. "Where did they go, Ox?" He lifted his eyes to the stars. "Up there?"

Oxley smiled tolerantly. "No, not into space..." Putting his palms together to form an X, he inverted his hands. "Into the space *between spaces*."

Mutt's eyebrows beetled. "I still don't get it. How did a legend about a city of gold spring up when there wasn't an ounce of it down there?"

Indy glanced at him. "The Ugha word for gold translates as 'treasure.' The Spaniards assumed that meant gold, when it actually referred to knowledge." He looked at Oxley. "Speaking of which, you never did explain how you got past the Nazcans at the cemetery, Ox."

Oxley merely shrugged. "I went during the day, when the warriors sleep. No one in their right mind would rob graves in broad daylight."

Indy laughed shortly and tipped his hat back. "I never thought of that."

Marion leaned over to touch Mutt's face. The gash Spalko's rapier had incised on his left cheek had reopened. "You're going to have a nasty scar."

"Plenty more where that came from," Indy said, groaning in pain as he leaned back against a tree.

Tilting his hat down over his forehead, he exhaled audibly and closed his eyes. Marion lowered her head to gaze up at him from beneath the brim of the fedora and managed to catch his eye before fatigue overcame him. He answered her smile with one of his own, and when he held an arm out for her, she crawled into his embrace and rested her head on his shoulder.

Mutt regarded everyone in bewilderment. "So we're just gonna sit here?"

"Night falls quickly in the jungle, kid," Indy said. "We can't climb down in the dark."

"Says who?"

Hearing Mutt get to his feet, Indy pushed his hat back and looked at him. "Why don't you stick around, Junior?"

Mutt shot him a look. "I don't know. Why didn't you, Dad?"

Indy raised his eyes to the stars. "Somewhere my old man is laughing."

Oxley glanced from Mutt to Indy and back again. "*Dad?*" he asked.

CHAPTER TWENTY-SIX

O n the campus of Marshall College, Dean Stanforth hurried down the hallway that led to his office, passing Indy's office en route, where a sign painter was at work amending the legend on the door's frosted glass panel. Previously the legend had read: *Henry Jones, Jr., Professor of Archaeology*, and the painter was putting the final touches on a new line.

Associate Dean.

Aware of Stanforth's stare, the painter turned from his work. "Am I doing something wrong?"

"No, carry on," Stanforth was quick to assure him. "By all means continue."

Hurrying his pace, Stanforth arrived at his office and went immediately to one of the tall bookcases, from which he retrieved a tattered edition of the Bible.

"A minister forgetting to bring a Bible," Stanforth muttered to himself. "What's the world coming to?"

*   *   *

Tapping his foot impatiently, Indy, dressed in a new suit and bowtie, stood at the front of the church, shoulder to shoulder with Marion, who wore a simple dress that complemented her natural beauty. Mutt was just behind his father, sporting a sharp suit and narrow tie. A somber but forgetful man, the minister held the Bible Dean Stanforth had delivered at the last minute.

Harold Oxley, back to being the buttoned-up academic Indy remembered, sat in one of the front pews, close to where Stanforth, his wife, Deirdre, and their two adult children were sitting. Behind them sat General Robert Ross, many of Indy's colleagues, and some of his students.

"Oh, how much human life is lost in waiting," Oxley said, loudly enough to elicit muted laughter from a few of the guests.

"But it is also a declaration of love," the minister was droning on. Opening the Bible, he added, "And now I wish to read to you what Paul wrote about love in a Letter to the Corinthians, who at the time were —"

Impulsively, Indy pulled Marion into his arms and kissed her full on the mouth.

"Jones!" Marion said in a muffled voice, pushing him away. "This is supposed to wait till the ceremony's finished."

"Finished?" Indy grinned lopsidedly. "Honey, I'm just getting warmed up."

When the inappropriate kiss resumed, some of the guests cheered, and Oxley shouted, "Well *done*, Henry!"

At the sound of the name, both Indiana and Mutt turned and spoke at the same time.

"Thanks, Ox."

Putting both arms around Marion, Indy began to kiss her again. Eyeing them with disapproval, the minister shut the Bible and went directly to the marriage vows.

Organ music began to waft from the small balcony, and attendants at the rear of the church threw open the wooden doors. A sudden breeze tugged Indy's fedora from a hat rack and sent it spinning down the center aisle, where it came to rest at the toes of a scuffed-up pair of motorcycle boots.

Mutt picked the hat up and dusted it off; then, after regarding it for a moment, raised it to his head, perhaps simply to see if it fit. The fedora was halfway to its intended destination when a hand reached out and snatched it from Mutt's grip.

Throwing Mutt a cautionary look and an affectionate grin, Indy put the hat where it belonged: atop his own head.